HOLDING HANDS

A NOVELLA

STEVIE TURNER

HOLDING HANDS

ISBN: 978-1-7394010-8-5

DEDICATION

To Ron.

TABLE OF CONTENTS

DESCRIPTION

Elderly widower Tom Hopkins is lonely. In-between going to Bingo, taking bus rides for the sake of it to look around shops, and trying line dancing for beginners, he often spends his time doing voluntary work as a hand-holder in the Ophthalmology Department of his local hospital where nervous people arrive to undergo injections for the eye condition 'wet age-related macular degeneration'

Ellen Wilkinson, also widowed, is a patient in the clinic. She soon makes a friend of Tom after they meet by chance in the hospital's café. Unbeknown to Tom, Ellen is a wealthy woman and has not yet made a will. Her son Bob is against the friendship, and tries his best to stop the burgeoning relationship between his mother and Tom.

When Bob finds out that a wedding might be on the cards, he is sure Tom is a gold-digger and is determined to stop the marriage once and for all. Ellen and Tom, however, have other ideas, but are unprepared for the lengths Bob will go in order to scupper their plans.

CHAPTER ONE

TOM

I can't look at the poor bastard as a Lucentis injection goes right into his eye. The bloke's terrified, but then so would *I* be if it were *me* lying on the slab. I can see his breathing increase as he clenches his fists. This is where I step in…I'm a bit wary of men's reactions though, but hey, his adrenaline's flowing and he'll probably think it's a nurse. I make a tentative reach for his fingers, and he grabs my hand and hangs on as though his life depends on it.

"You're doing fine." I try to make my voice as reassuring as possible. "Soon be over."

I don't stroke the fingers, mind you, not even with the ladies. There's nothing sexual in my intentions at all. I'm just doing a bit of voluntary work on Mondays and Thursdays now that I'm too ancient to be of use to anybody else. I'm fit and healthy, but I'll be eighty seven next muck spreading. The patients who are more 'with it' sometimes give me a second look as if they're wondering why on earth such an old codger as I obviously am is still working in a medical treatment room, but then they have to lie down under the spotlight for a needle full of Lucentis and their minds go to mush. If somebody like me holds their hand, then I've found majority of them seem very grateful for it.

The chap whose hand I'm holding looks as though he might pass out with fright. My fingers feel numb under his grip until the injection is over. Then he relaxes, catches sight of me, and wrenches his hand away as though I've just escaped from a leper colony. I don't mind; many of them do the same. I'm just a temporary oasis in a desert of meddling medics. Once their injection is over, patients can't get away fast enough, especially from me. I suppose I remind them of their moment of weakness.

After ten or so injections it's time for a break. I've lived on my own since Jean died, and it's somewhat daunting to walk into a tea room full of doctors, nurses and secretaries all at least thirty years younger than I am and all talking nineteen to the dozen. Sometimes there isn't even a seat, and so I have to stand. Today the urn of hot water bubbles away; I take a tea bag and somebody's cup who is off sick today, and hope I don't fall arse over tit over a pair of outstretched legs as I make my way towards the fridge for a drop of milk.

"Okay, Tom?"

The only person who occasionally speaks to me is Rachel, one of the secretaries. I stir my tea and head towards the only seat that's left.

"So far, so good." I sit down and try not to make the 'old man' noise. "It's the weekend tomorrow anyway."

"Those cakes on the table are for my birthday." Rachel points towards a box of chocolate eclairs. "Help yourself. They won't last long."

"Thanks." I feel guilty as I reach over and grab one. "Happy birthday."

Rachel is nice. The others are too high up the food chain to bother with a volunteer worker, especially one who is pushing ninety. I chomp away at an éclair and hope my dentures aren't moving too much. To be honest, it's easier to eat without them, and when I'm at home I often do.

I endure feeling like a fish out of water for a further ten minutes whilst everyone either stares at their mobile phones or chats to each other. I decide I don't want to interrupt their conversations with pointless small talk they probably won't be interested in. Rachel goes back to work, and so that puts the kybosh on any possible human interaction. I get up and head for the lavatory, relieved to stand at the urinal in perfect peace.

I decide to wait in the treatment room for Doctor, no *Mister*, Joseph, one of the ophthalmic surgeons, to return after his break. On the way I pass a sea of expectant faces, each one as miserable as patients in a pox doctor's waiting room. Some of them I recognise due to the amount of injections they've had before, but others are terrified newbies. I feel for them all.

As usual Mister Joe is late, simply because he *can* be. I know the patients will be shifting about and clucking in frustration, but there's no point in trying to hurry him up. He'll amble along in his own sweet time, a tinpot king of the clinic. A full thirty minutes after he should have started, Mister Joe rolls up, gives me a condescending glance, scrolls through the first set of notes on the computer, and throws a few curt words in the direction of the treatment room nurse.

"Send Ellen Wilkinson in."

A 'please' would have gone down better. From the way the nurse shoots him an evil eye, I can tell *she* doesn't care for him either. I much prefer working with Miss Rose, who has more than her fair share of empathy. Perhaps she needs to give this arsehole of a surgeon some of it.

A lady obviously in her early eighties hobbles into the treatment room with the aid of a walking frame. I give her my widest smile and place my old carcass on a seat parallel to the middle of the operating table opposite to where Mister Joe and the nurse will do their thing. I can see he's already impatient at the elderly woman's lack of speed, and I want to shout out to him that one day *he'll* be old too, but hey, he's *God*, and gods live forever on an elixir of eternal youth and their own self-importance. The patient takes a consent form from the nurse with shaky fingers, signs it, and then listens to a list of side effects and what not to do afterwards. She nods, lies down on the operating table, and I grasp her hand, which feels cold.

"Won't take long. It'll be over in a jiffy."

"I hope so."

Mrs Wilkinson is quite well spoken, stoic, and with her ongoing mobility difficulties has obviously learned to endure. I don't squeeze her fingers, as that smacks of familiarity. The nurse faffs around the bed and decides to be the first to break the silence.

"Mister Joseph will numb your eye first, and then inject it with Lucentis."

So far the surgeon hasn't said a word. He must be having a bad day. Mrs Wilkinson's hand warms up under my grasp. It feels soft, as though she hasn't had a lifetime of hard work, but some of the fingers are knobbly with arthritis. I can recall hands more than faces now; fat ones, thin ones, long fingers, stubby fingers, some with wedding rings and some without.

"Yes, that's what he said at my first clinic appointment, plus the fact it will keep new blood vessels from forming under the retina."

I can't look at her face, because that means I'd see the needle going in. I don't care too much for needles. I concentrate on the blue patterned blanket and hope my presence is bringing some kind of comfort, albeit small. The faces may change, but it's the hands I remember.

CHAPTER TWO

I still haven't got used to going home to an empty flat, and I guess I never will. Jean died more than a year ago now. Sometimes when loneliness gets too much for me I open her wardrobe, as I'm going to do now. Her clothes have gone of course, but her perfume seems to have sunk into the wood and it lingers on inside. Often, like today, I'll step inside the wardrobe, pull the door to, and stand there in the darkness with my memories. We never had any children, but just being together for 65 years was enough for us. The trouble with getting to such an advanced age is that all our relatives have died, apart from a niece of Jean's who lives on the mainland and whom I never see. I'm an only child, and so that makes things worse.

It's comforting inside Jean's wardrobe; I don't want to come out. We did not have a cross word in all our married life, and even when Jean failed to conceive month after month, we agreed never to take any tests in order to discover whose fault it was, just in case we blamed each other for the lack of babies. Jean pursued her career as a nurse, eventually moving up the scale to Matron, which did much to satisfy her need to look after people. Me, I worked as a roofer, and it kept me fit going up and down those ladders for years on end. The knees couldn't do it anymore now, but I've still got all my original joints even if they don't work as well as they once did. Plus the fact that Jean was an excellent cook, and she never served up what they call 'junk' food nowadays; plenty of vegetables and fruit was her motto.

She always thought that if we ate well then she might fall pregnant.

We were a team; Jean cooked and I washed the dishes afterwards. She still insisted on cooking even when riddled with cancer and half doped up with pain medication, but the doctor told me to let her do whatever she was able to. I had to hover close by just in case she let the saucepans boil over or switched on one of the hobs over the steamer, and in this way I finally learned how to cook. Trouble is, most days I can't be bothered to cook just for one, and stick a ready meal in the microwave instead.

It's Tuesday today. I'm not needed at the hospital as there's no injection clinics until Thursday. So far I've avoided Bingo in the community hall, but today is a bad day and I think I'll have to toddle along and give it a go. You'd think that living in a sheltered housing complex as I do there would be lots of people to talk to, but they're either asleep all the afternoon, at the hospital or the doctors' surgery, or they've dropped dead and their flat is empty. Did you know there's a dedicated ambulance space out by our main entrance? What could have been a covered parking space for motorbikes around the back is now more often than not full of mobility scooters.

Needs must, and I cannot stay in this flat a moment longer. I lock my front door and venture out into the corridor, which is as quiet as the grave. No… I mustn't mention graves… I've already got one foot in that. Hey ho… will there be anybody alive in the community hall? Jean felt safe and secure in this complex and made quite a few friends, but her friends were all women. I've nothing against the female sex, but being a roofer for all those years I became used to the type of banter you can only find in male company. All the husbands are dead here, killed off by too many fried breakfasts or cheesy chips, and I'm the only fella. Jean fed me well, which has kept me alive, but hey, what's the point of living when the love of your life has gone?

***

Five women sit nattering at a table, Bingo dabbers in their hands. The prizes are lined up in their entirety; two tins of soup of indeterminate age, a six-pack bag of cheesy Doritos, a Toblerone, and a hideous turtle thing with a nodding head. I don't fancy winning any of those. Too late, I realise I should have brought a prize. Warden Penny smiles and looks me up and down from her desk, as do the ladies.

"Nice to see you here, Tom. We haven't seen you around much."

"I've been volunteering at the hospital." I stand awkwardly in the doorway. "It keeps me out of mischief."

"Well, come and sit down. I've got a spare dabber."

"You can get some ointment for that."

Nobody titters. I take a seat at an empty table away from the women in case they think I fancy any of them (I'd rather have a hot dinner). Bingo turns out to be excruciatingly boring, as I knew it would be. I win the last game and end up with a prize that nobody else wanted… the nodding turtle.

By four o'clock I'm back in the flat and heat up a ready meal for something to do. I know I'll be hungry again before I go to bed and will need to grab a sandwich, but hey… who cares if I put on a few pounds? Jean would have told me to miss out on a few lunches, but I don't need to look good for anyone now and so I can please myself.

The nodding turtle stares at me from Jean's side of the table. The shepherd's pie tastes good and I don't need to use my teeth. I balance my top row on the turtle's head and its eyes sink down wards, unable now to reproach me after I accompany my meal with a couple of cans of lager rather than Jean's usual glass of water. A big lump of supermarket cherry pie finishes me off, and I'm ready for a snooze. The washing up can wait.

It's not until eight o'clock that I get around to washing the dishes. I could kick myself for sleeping for so long, because now I know I'll be tossing and turning all night. I tend to take naps whenever I can, and really it's just to escape the sad reality of my situation. I used to play Chess, Scrabble or Trivial Pursuit with Jean; I would win more Chess games, and she would more often than not beat me soundly at Scrabble and Trivial Pursuit. We'd enjoy competing, but with Jean's superior vocabulary and general knowledge it was a no-brainer who would usually be the victor. The old girls living here at the complex seem brain-addled. All I have left to keep Alzheimer's disease from knocking on my door are my books of Sudoku puzzles and the Daily Mail crossword.

It's quarter to nine and I'm wide awake after my nap. I switch on the TV and flick through a few channels, settling on a Western starring John Wayne as an elderly rancher having to herd cattle 400 miles to Belle Fourche with only the help of a team of young boys. What the hell… he's pushing 60 in this film… I'm 27 years older than he is! If he's elderly, then what am I? Methuselah reincarnated?

The film takes me out of myself for a while, and stops me staring at the empty armchair where Jean would sit and knit or crochet. I fall into bed at midnight and stare at the ceiling for an hour before slipping into dreamland.

CHAPTER THREE

Wednesday mornings, and it's line dancing for beginners in the village hall. Yes, even *I*, dancing like Douglas Bader after a night out on the piss, can join in, as you don't need a partner. I pay my three pounds and look around the hall. Once again it's all the same middle aged or elderly women, and the only man is Donald, tall, willowy and slightly stooped, who takes the class and teaches us the steps. His wife Mary is maybe in her late seventies and dances with us. I think Donald is either the same age as me, or even older (if that's possible). He wears a cowboy shirt with fringes, drainpipe jeans, and the same natty pair of grey Cuban heeled boots every week. He's as bald as a coot. I think they live about twenty miles away in Newport. That's Newport on the Isle of Wight by the way, not the one in Welsh Wales.

Now Donald might have been an ace line dancer in his prime, but his old brain isn't as quick as it used to be and he keeps forgetting where he is in the dance. He gets mixed up with his jazz boxes, grapevines, turns and shuffles, and then we all end up facing different directions. Mary soon puts him right though, but then he'll have a sulk because she's had to tell him what to do. In my opinion he's a complete arsehole, and I don't know how she's lived with him all these years. But hey, it's somewhere to go and something to do.

Donald doesn't like me. Perhaps being the only other male in the room he sees me as some kind of threat. Well… yeah, I *can* be threatening if he starts shouting at me because I do a kickball change by mistake instead of a jazz box, but sometimes Mary yells at him that it *should* be a kickball change, so then I gloat and stand victorious. Silly old bugger. He takes it all far too seriously. If I want to do a kickball change, then I will.

I stand and watch when it comes to the faster ones, as the legs refuse to do them anymore. Donald has trouble as well, but he likes being in charge and unfortunately won't give up. Mary can do the steps much better than *he* can, and to be honest it's easier to follow her lead instead of his. Donald wears a headset with a microphone attached, just like one of those boy bands you see on TV. His booming bass voice belts out which steps to do, but after a few weeks I've learned to shut him off and copy Mary. I think the other women do too, but I don't dare speak to them too much in case they think I'm a pervert.

After half an hour of dancing it's time for a cup of tea. I always offer to help, but the women take over and usher me out of the kitchen. I sit on my own, as far away from Donald as I can manage. The tea is weak, like cats' piss. I get one biscuit as well for my three pounds.

The last few dances after the break are slower, as we're all old and knackered. Too late … I coaster when I should have done a mambo.

"Keep up, Tom." Donald and his headset whip around to stare at me. "I'm sure I said *mambo*."

I want to tell him to shove his mambo up his arse, but then Mary clucks around me like an old mother hen.

"You're doing fine. We all make mistakes sometimes."

Trying to remember which step comes next is good for me though, as it keeps my brain from going soft. When I'm dancing I forget Jean is no longer with me, as I'm too busy to think about her. As soon as the class ends there she is again, in the back of my mind.

I enjoy a slow walk back along Steyne Road. A couple of the other women from the class live in my complex, and they chat away together as they walk a few yards in front of me. My legs ache after all that dancing, and I can't keep up. I pass the supermarket, and then take a detour into Bembridge's small cemetery for a while, where my wife is buried.

"Hello old girl. It's me." I take a seat right by Jean's grave. "You'll laugh, but I've been line dancing again."

Birds trill their songs in the midday sun, and a heat haze shimmers over Jean's headstone. I look at an empty space underneath the bit where it says Jean Hopkins fell asleep on 5th March 2023, and feel sorry that Jean's niece will have the job of getting my own name added underneath. Still, at least she won't have to pay for anything…I've made sure of that.

I talk about everything and nothing to Jean, and feel better after a rest and a chat, even though the conversation is rather one-sided. I get to my feet and carry on along Steyne Road, and then turn right along Egerton Road towards the retirement complex and Wednesday's community lunch of the usual toad-in-the-hole with veggies and then sponge pudding and custard for afters. I can cope with that. Okay, so I have to sit with the other residents as they dribble and drool all over their food, but it's better than cooking it myself even though they do charge me for it at the end of the month. Any company is better than none, and hey, sometimes one can become rather tired of all those ready meals.

Line dancing makes you hungry… well, it does *me* anyway. Warden Penny and a couple of helpers serve up the food and pots of tea as we sit at tables of four. I'm stuck with Cissie, Ethel and Edie, none of whom can hear as well as they used to.

"I didn't see you ladies at line dancing today."

"What?" Ethel's blank stare is a vision to behold.

"He said this tea tastes like urine." Edie takes a gulp of tea and frowns.

I shake my head at Edie, who tends to make it all up as she goes along. Sometimes it's funny, and sometimes it isn't. I wolf down my lunch, eager to get away from them all.

Back at my flat I join in with the usual activity here after lunch… a snooze. Sleeping whiles away the next two hours and makes the day feel a bit shorter. I stretch out on the sofa and give a gentle sigh. At least I won't have to cook a meal tonight and can just get by with a pile of sandwiches. Sometimes I can't be bothered with all this domestic stuff. I think I must be getting lazy in my old age.

CHAPTER FOUR

The bus is on time, and very soon I'm on my way to St. Jude's Hospital in Newport. I'm glad Miss Rose is working in the eye clinic today. Sara Rose is patience and kindness personified, and the old dears love her. She even has time for *me*, and asks what I've been doing all week. I'm sure she's not interested in Bingo or line dancing, but anyway, she always sounds as though she is.

Another round of hand holding begins. The temperature outside has risen to 30 degrees Centigrade, and there's no air conditioning in the treatment room. I'm often cold in my old age, but not today, and I hope the patients aren't put off by my sweaty hands. At least I get to wash them in-between patients, which of course is only right and proper.

I do recognise some of the faces, as the same patients often come back for a course of injections. Some of them crack jokes and seem overly happy, but I suppose that's because they're nervous. One chap even asked Mister Joe if he'd ever wanted to be a train driver when he was a little boy, just when he was about to stick the needle in. Mister Joe has no sense of humour at all, and so the question ended up lost in the ether.

Miss Rose always brings a CD player to her Thursday clinics and puts on some music, usually middle-of-the-road songs that are soothing. Today it's something different; a selection of classical music. Jean often played classical music, but it's not my cup of tea. However, I recognise the next tune… it's one that Jean used to try and play on our old piano years ago, before arthritis set in and caused her fingers to stiffen and go out of shape.

"What's this one called?" I grasp the patient's hand a little bit tighter. Now I don't know who is comforting whom.

"It's 'Für Elise', by Beethoven." Miss Rose's soft voice breaks into my reverie. "Do you like it?"

I cannot reply. The music washes over me, bringing with it wave after wave of painful memories. The patient wriggles her fingers a little, and I loosen my grip.

"Sorry."

My vision is swimming, and with a free hand I wipe away some telltale tears. I'm glad I'm looking away from the business end, as I wouldn't want anybody to see me in such an emotional state. I make a mental note to visit the high street in the near future and see if I can buy that tune. I let go of the patient's hand as soon as the injection is over, get to my feet, and make my way over to the double sink. Miss Rose's eagle eyes have not missed a thing unfortunately. She takes off her gloves and turns the hot tap on with her elbow.

"Are you okay, Tom?"

I was hoping to feel a bit more composed before I had to answer. All I can do is nod.

"It'll get better with time."

They must have been speaking about me in the tea room. I hate everyone knowing my business, but you can't ignore the questions they ask. Yes, they sympathise, but they're all younger and don't really know what it's like to lose your life partner.

"I know." I scrub my hands a little too hard. "It's only been fifteen months."

"No time at all. Keep busy, Tom, and thanks for all your help here. I know the patients are very grateful."

I make a great show of drying my hands, and feel a bit more composed as the next patient comes in. It's a big hairy bloke about thirty years younger than me, and I'm a little wary as I tentatively hold his hand. He snatches it away, and that's my cue to sit still and keep my hands to myself. Not all patients want a stranger reaching out and grasping their fingers, especially men, and I have to accept that.

The clinic is over by half past four, and I eke out the afternoon by making a stop in the hospital's café for a jacket potato and salad before walking out to the bus stop near the front entrance. One good thing about living on the Isle of Wight is that you can rely on the *Vectis* bus service – I long ago gave up driving as it's cheaper to use my free bus pass, even if the bus does go all around the houses and take forever to get anywhere. Never mind… I've got all the time in the world. I tap my card against the machine (whatever happened to bus conductors?), and think about Jean during the 45 minutes it takes to get back to Steyne Road.

First left down Egerton Road is Brooks Close. I did the roof of number 20 when I was younger and fitter. There used to be an old lady living there, but maybe she's now in sheltered housing just like me or has shuffled off to Buffalo. She used to give me tea and biscuits every couple of hours; I was up and down that ladder like a blue arse fly. I crane my neck to see down to the end of the road, but as usual, nobody's about.

There's a smell of boiled cabbage as I enter the complex. A few more hours to fill, and then I can go to bed.

CHAPTER FIVE

I like Fridays. One of the carers takes me in her car to Tesco's at Ryde and helps me to do my weekly shop. I have to pay her of course, but Doreen is good company and we have a bit of a laugh. I don't pay her outright, but the amount I owe goes onto an invoice which is presented to me at the end of the month, along with bills for any lunches I've had and also whether I've had a haircut from the mobile hairdresser or a visit from the travelling chiropodist. Sometimes Doreen takes another resident to Tesco as well, but today I can see there'll only be the two of us.

Doreen is eternally cheerful. Whether this is for my benefit or she's like that anyway I cannot tell. I expect nothing nasty has ever happened to Doreen to make her miserable. She's about 55 at a guess, and married with three grown up kids. Life holds no pitfalls for Doreen, and sometimes this fills me with jealousy. Why should the likes of Doreen have it easy, while others have more of a bumpy ride? The answer, of course, is *why not*? I fit my tall frame down into Doreen's half pint car with some difficulty, and wish for the umpteenth time that I could still afford to drive myself about.

"Hey Tom, how's it going today?"

"Don't know, it's a bit early yet." I clutch a few empty carrier bags as though my life depends on it. "I'll tell you later."

Doreen drives as though she's racing at Silverstone. I never feel too safe on our Tesco runs, but there's no way I can carry all my shopping home without her. People say learn how to order stuff on the internet, but it's like a foreign language to me. I didn't grow up with computers, and so far have managed to live nearly 90 years without using one. I think that's no mean feat nowadays. The same goes for mobile phones… what the hell do I want one for? My relatives are all dead except one niece, and we now only exchange birthday and Christmas cards; the few friends I do have are at the complex. All I've got is my post office account where my pensions go into. The post office is just a short walk away in Steyne Road, and I can queue up when it opens and get money out for shopping if I need to. I can ask for a balance and they'll print one for me. I'm happy with that.

It's not too far to Tesco. Doreen natters on about nothing in particular, while I notice that I can't quite see the registration number of the car in front of me while the sun is shining on it. Glare obscures my vision, but as soon as we stop in the shade at traffic lights I can see quite clearly again. I've never noticed this before. Perhaps it was just a one-off thing.

"You're quiet this morning."

"Sorry Doreen, I was miles away."

"Thinking about Jean?"

"I suppose." I nod. "Sometimes I still can't believe she's gone."

"I felt like that too when my first husband died."

I come back to reality with a bump, as I'd had no idea that Doreen had been married before.

"Your first husband died? He must have been young."

"Sure… only thirty four. I'd not long had my third child. Accident at work. I gave him a lunch box, said I'd see him later, but the next time I *did* see him he was laid out in the hospital mortuary."

"Good God." I feel a twinge of guilt for being so self-pitying. "I didn't know."

"Hey, I went through those five stages of grief a long time ago. I met Malcolm and we've been married for ten years now."

We arrive at the end of the Beaper Shute. Doreen turns right into the road leading to Tesco.

"I've heard of those stages. How long? I mean… how long to get through them?"

"As long as it takes, Tom. We're all different. You'll know when you're at the last one."

"Which is?"

"Acceptance".

Doreen parks the car and as I get out of the passenger seat I realise to my dismay that I'm still in the early stages. I sometimes think that Jean's going to walk through our front door. It's as though the shock of her death hasn't yet sunk in. If only I could have persuaded her to go to the GP as soon as she noticed the first symptoms, but she was like me… I tend to gloss over any illness and hope it goes away. So far it has, but it didn't for Jean.

Tesco is always busy in the summer months. Holidaymakers come here straight from the ferry and stock up on goodies for their caravans or hotel rooms. I pass by the vacancy notice board, and realise I'm too old and knackered for any of the jobs advertised. I look at happy young families as they load up their trollies, and feel pangs of jealousy. My life is finished. All I'm doing now is just eking out the days until I can be with Jean again. But at least I have Doreen to help me. She's good to me and I mustn't keep going on about my problems to her. Nobody wants to think about death, and in particular they're not interested in other people's grief. People have enough troubles of their own. Would I want some old boy keep on nattering at *me* about his dead wife? No, I wouldn't, so I need to shut up.

Mum always told me to treat people how I would want to be treated, and she was right.

The weekend ahead looms long, loathsome and lonely.

CHAPTER SIX

There's always the Vectis bus rides to save my sanity. On Saturdays I walk down to Steyne Road and board the bus for another free ride to Newport, but this time instead of going to the eye clinic I have a look around the shops. There's usually nothing I need to buy, but it's nice to see young people who aren't old or sick. Sometimes I get a haircut by the Turkish barber instead of the mobile hairdresser at the home, and he asks me how the Island used to be in days gone by.

I'm a creature of habit, and while I'm in Newport on Saturdays I like to have my lunch in The Blue Door Café. It's small and cosy and the ladies who run the café are talkative and friendly. I always order a ham omelette and salad. Now it's summertime I know the big windows will be open, and if I'm lucky enough to get a corner seat I can watch the world go by while I eat. I'm on first name terms with the café's ladies now, as I've had my lunch in there almost every Saturday since Jean died.

So it's Saturday again today and it's half past eleven. Where else to go but The Blue Door? There's already families seated outside, but as usual I hurry inside and hope the tables aren't all taken. Diane plonks a Victoria sponge on the counter and then raises one hand.

"Hello Tom."

Diane will never know how eternally grateful I am for that greeting. She might be the only person I'll speak to all day, and so I'm going to make the most of it.

"'Morning, Diane. Busy?"

"Of course… the weather's good." Diane chuckles and places a net-like protector over the sponge. "But we wouldn't have it any other way. The usual for you?"

"Maybe it's time for something different." I look up at the menu on the wall above Diane's head. "How about a sausage sandwich on white bread and a cup of tea?"

"You little devil, you! Coming right up. There's one table left inside."

It's not a window seat, but instead a table for two right next to the toilet door. It's not my preferred choice. I sit down and face the wall rather than having to look at my fellow diners, who all seem immersed in their phones and therefore uncommunicative. I'm not sure what the attraction is in continually staring at phones… people do it all the time and it annoys the hell out of me. Whatever happened to conversation?

One of the Saturday girls brings my sandwich and then walks away again, without me even having the chance to thank her. It's difficult to eat with my teeth in, and I take my time. After I've finished I sip my tea and take a quick glance around the room. The window seat I like is free and so I move over to it, relieved not to have to stare at the wall anymore. I focus on shoppers going past in the street outside, and relax a little bit more. The Saturday girl hurries by and collects my empty plate.

"Could I have some of that lovely Victoria sponge and another cup of tea please?"

I'm happy I'm in the right seat. I could stay here all afternoon, but they're busy and they want the table. I stay as long as I can.

Around the corner from the café is Waterstones, with its rows of brand new books. I love the smell of a new book. There's even a couple of chairs so I can eke out the time until the 3pm bus arrives and read a paragraph or two, but I must be careful and not be tempted to buy anything. I have a whole shelf of books not yet read just because I've lingered too long in Waterstones over the past year or so. I can't seem to sit at home and concentrate for any length of time on a story, and I don't know why. I'm happier when I'm out of the complex, maybe because indoors there's Jean's empty chair opposite mine. I keep looking at it instead reading the book.

About twenty past two it's time to make my way to the bus station. Granted I'm not the fastest person, but everyone's in such a hurry along the high street, and some bump me with their bags of shopping. I take my time and reach the bus stop around ten to three. A couple of elderly ladies stand there and I say hello. We chat about the weather, and I make the most of it because I know that apart from the warden's regular phone call to check I'm not dead, I'll speak to nobody else tomorrow until I get to St. Jude's eye clinic on Monday afternoon.

The bus arrives. There's quite a queue behind me now, and I know most of the seats will get taken as people finish their shopping and head for home. An old boy plonks himself next to me, and we end up putting the world to rights in the hour or so it takes to get back to Bembridge. He gets off the bus a couple of stops before I do, and I return home feeling happier and more energized. I haven't seen him before, but I hope to see him again next week. I don't even know what his name is, as blokes don't worry about things like that. Perhaps if we travel on the same bus for a second time I could suggest going to some pub for a beer or two. He could be as lonely as I am, but neither of us would ever broach this subject; too personal. It almost feels shameful that I've got nobody at home (or anywhere else for that matter) to give two hoots about me. It's not something you want to go around announcing in a loud voice.

A nap will fill a few more hours until dinner. I close my eyes and think of my 'mates'; those guys with strong arms and legs they got through carrying full hods of bricks or roof tiles up and down ladders all day. Where are they now? All dead due to excesses; smoking, drinking and eating too much fat and sugar. One by one they all withered away and died off, and I'm the only one over eighty five still left alive. I think I've been to more funerals than anyone else in this world. Not much of an accolade, is it?

By the time Sunday comes around I'm even thinking of attending the local church service. At least I'll see people there who might even talk to me. I've never been that much of a God-botherer to be honest, just weddings and aforesaid funerals, that's me. It seems a bit hypocritical to turn up though. He'll know I'm only there for the company, and so will the vicar. The congregation will all stare and wonder who the old boy sitting at the back is. Nah… it's only one day. I'll get by. I might even wander along the corridor and mend Cissie's toaster if I get really desperate. She'll bend my ear for as long as it takes me to get out of the door again. Hmm…thinking about it... no.

CHAPTER SEVEN

ONE MONTH LATER

I'm a bit early for the eye clinic, and so I make my way up to the café for a cup of tea and a sticky bun before I start. Jean used to brainwash me about not eating too much sugar, but hey, she's not here anymore to keep an eye on what I'm doing. I've got to have a bit of comfort food in my old age and I've have slipped up more times recently than I care to remember, with the result that now my trousers are a bit tight and I've had to undo a notch or two on my belt.

I find just one empty table to sit at on my own. It's not possible to face a wall because the table is in the middle of the café. I've always found it strange how people sit around tables near the walls first and only then use the middle tables if there are no other ones around the edge, but I do this myself and so I can't blame anyone else for doing the same. Perhaps it's something to do with the primitive urge to feel safe from invaders.

I bite into my sticky bun. It tastes good. I mentally apologise to Jean and then wash the bun down with a swig of tea. It's only then that I feel a tap on my shoulder.

"Excuse me. You're the man in the eye clinic, aren't you?"

I swallow what's left of the bun, and look round. An elderly woman walking with the aid of a frame comes into my visual field. She wears a pair of black trousers, a pink top that comes down over her hips, and a pair of those slip on Velcro shoes that

I told myself I'd never wear but actually do. She's got short grey hair and is unremarkable in every way. I'm sure I've never seen her before.

"Er… yes, I do voluntary work there twice a week. In fact I'll be working there today when I've finished my tea."

"I thought so." The woman nodded. "My appointment's at ten past two. I'm Ellen…Mrs Wilkinson. Remember me? I have Lucentis injections in my eye every month, and you always hold my hand."

"Do I?"

I've held so many hands that after a while they become disembodied. I take a sip of tea and try not to stare too hard at the woman's face, which definitely doesn't look familiar.

"Yes, and I'm very grateful for it. Call me Ellen. Can I sit at your table, please? My son had to drop me off early, and there's no other seats. The girl's going to bring my cup over in a minute. I can't carry it and use a frame at the same time."

"Well, of course." I indicate towards one of the empty chairs. "Be my guest."

It's a nice change to have another person at my table. Somebody brings Ellen some tea and a complimentary biscuit, and she dips the biscuit in her tea.

"You don't mind, do you?" She pops the biscuit into her mouth. "After all, we're not at the Ritz."

"I do that myself at home." I chuckle at her lack of airs and graces. "Carry on."

I'm ready to start my duties, but now am reluctant to leave the café before Ellen does.

"I'm Tom, by the way. I just do voluntary work here on Mondays and Thursdays. It gets me out of the house."

"And good on you, Tom… you're doing a grand job."

I've never thought much about the people whose hands I hold. As I said, they're just hands; some warm, some cold, some sweaty, some clammy. Lo and behold, now there's a real person opposite me whom I know hardly at all and whose hands I've already held and whose hands I've got to hold again in a very short while. I don't really want to associate hands with people, as I expect it might be embarrassing for both of us. Nevertheless, today I've got to do it.

The overhead lights are too bright for me, and I'm eager to be on my way. I check the clock on the far wall, but find that some of the numbers are obscured as though there's a net curtain in the way.

"I'd better go." I squint at the clock. "What time do you make it?"

"Quarter to two by my watch."

"Strange." I move my chair out, glance at the clock again, and get ready to stand up. "I used to be able to see that clock, but now it's like someone's painted out a few of the numbers."

"That's how *my* macular deterioration started." Ellen nods. "Not being able to read properly if bright lights or bright sunshine shone on a page or on a sign."

I stay fixed in my chair for a moment to let the irony of the situation sink in.

"So there am I helping patients in the eye clinic, but now I'm in the same boat as *they* are?"

"Shit happens." Ellen shrugs. "Why should *you* be any different to the rest of us? I've had mine since I was seventy one, and that's ten years ago."

I try not to laugh at her remark, which surprises me as it seems a little out of character.

"I suppose I'd better visit the GP then." I stand up. "By the way, you're still a spring chicken. You're six years younger than me."

"Tom, my mum always told me never to get old, and she was right. She also said to never get old and fat. I can't do much about getting old, but I *can* make sure I don't put on too much weight."

"Well done. See you in a while, anyway."

I leave Ellen at the table and make my way as quickly as I can to the eye clinic. The clocks are bigger there and easier to read, and it's just on two by the time I get there, but as usual King Joe hasn't arrived. I slide into my seat next to the operating table while the nurse bustles around getting patients' notes in order and preparing instruments. By the time Joe rolls up, Ellen would have been waiting twenty minutes past her appointment time. I say nothing in greeting. He totally ignores me anyway, and indicates towards the door.

"Nurse, you can send the first one in. Can I have their notes?"

A 'please' would have gone down well. The nurse must be from the agency, as I haven't seen her before. She seems a bit flustered. She runs towards Joe with a set of notes, and then hurries out the door. The first patient of the afternoon comes in; a vastly overweight man who has difficulty climbing on to the table. Joe switches on a bright light above the patient's head, and I tentatively reach out to touch the man's hand. Unsurprisingly he snatches his fingers away, and so I sit in silence and mind my own business.

At ten to three it's Ellen's turn. She gives me a smile as she enters the treatment room, and reaches out for my hand as soon as she is on the operating table. Her hand feels warm but creaky, and I make an assumption that arthritis has already set in. She squeezes my fingers, but I don't reciprocate as…er… well…I wasn't expecting this and I feel a bit awkward to tell you the truth. I'm not sure what to do. She's the one holding *my* hand now, rather than the other way around.

After her injection Ellen shuffles off the table, helped by the nurse. When she reaches the door she turns around and grins at me.

"See you again next month, Tom."

I'm flabbergasted. No patient in the clinic has ever said something like that to me before. It's easy to remember Ellen's features; they're imprinted in my brain now. I cannot help but to return her grin with one of my own. I feel like I'm 16 again.

CHAPTER EIGHT

I can't face Bingo today, and I don't want to stand in Jean's wardrobe. I'm not lonely though, and instead feel strangely uplifted for a change. It's a cool morning with a hint of autumn in the air, and I step outside just after half past nine to have a chat with my wife. My usual bench in the cemetery is empty, and early sunshine beams down upon her grave. A single red rose, still with dew on it, lies forlorn on the grass. I pick it up and place it on the top of Jean's tombstone, then sit down have a quick look around to make sure nobody else is about.

"Hello, old girl, I had a bit of a strange day yesterday, but knowing you I expect you've already guessed what I'm going to say."

A pigeon flies down onto the grass in front of me, pecks up some grass cuttings, and flies back off to its nest. The silence around me is almost palpable. I need to explain myself.

"There's nothing funny going on, she was just grateful of a hand to hold. She said she'll see me in a month's time when she has another appointment. She came up to *me* in the café, and not the other way around. I couldn't ignore her, could I?"

A lone car goes past on Steyne Road. The pigeon, whether it's the same one, coos from its nest somewhere up in a nearby yew tree. A photo of Jean, happy on our fiftieth wedding anniversary, adorns an oval glass inset near the top of the gravestone. I stare at her laughing eyes.

"There'll never be another lady like you. I carry you in my heart." I tap my chest. "Nobody will ever come between us."

I like to think that somewhere Jean can hear me and might even be able to see me sitting on the bench. The shell of her body lies under the ground, but not her spirit. One day I'll meet her in the afterlife, and she'll be the 20 year old girl that I fell in love with at first sight. Until then I'm prepared to have a one-sided conversation for however long it takes for us to be together again.

Jean doesn't answer of course, but the pigeon carries on cooing and the world turns as it should. I could easily light a cigarette now, but I gave up smoking thirty years ago. If truth be told I want to know why I'm so unsettled this morning, but deep down I think I might already have an idea… it was the shock of Ellen grabbing hold of my fingers yesterday. Patients don't usually do that, as they take my lead and either let me carry on or snatch their hand away. This rather brazen act from Ellen puts a whole new slant on things, and I can only conclude that her action makes me feel as though I'm not in control of the situation.

Well…*what to do*? Jean sulks and refuses to answer and to be honest, I'm stumped. Do I stay away from the clinic when Ellen is next due in? I enjoy my little job, and so … why should I? And here's another problem… I enjoyed the feel of another person squeezing my fingers, even though I'm pushing ninety. I'm in a right mucking fuddle (as my late brother used to say), and yes, I also feel guilty; guilty for thinking about Ellen while I'm sitting next to my wife's grave. The callow youth who went out with two girls at the same time seventy years ago has long ago seen the error of his ways. I learned a hard lesson from the one that wasn't Jean, and also from Jean herself when she found out and ditched me for Ernest Redmond, my best friend at the time. It took me one whole year to win her back, and of course I lost Ernie's friendship in the process.

But hey… Jean is no longer alive. I've been left on my own, and to be honest, as I've said before, there's nobody here who cares whether I live or die. I'll tell you, this loneliness takes a bit of getting used to. Ellen's small act of kindness is a beacon of light in an otherwise black existence. Yes, I'm looking forward to seeing her again, maybe in the hospital café where we can chat over another cup of tea. If a friendship develops from that, then all to the good. I would not have taken up voluntary work if Jean had still been living, and so the whole scenario would never have developed. However, I still feel a pang of guilt as I stand up and take one last look at the grave.

"Sorry, old girl, but it doesn't mean I don't love you. I *do*. You *know* that. It's just that this old boy is no good without you. He needs somebody to talk to."

The pigeon flaps its wings and flies away. I have a slow walk home and think about eating some corned beef and pickle sandwiches for lunch with a slice of lemon cake to follow.

CHAPTER NINE

I see her straight away as I check out who's sitting where in the hospital café. Ellen obviously arrived even earlier than I did, and I'm here over an hour before clinic starts at 2pm. I got the 12:10 bus, but at the moment don't want to deal with the fact that when going along and looking out of the bus window I found it impossible to read the signposts while the sun shone directly upon them.

Ellen looks up from pouring tea and gives me a wave. Before I've decided whether or not I should be so presumptuous as to sit myself down at her table, she points to me and then to an empty chair beside her. I nod and take my place in the lunchtime queue, all the while as nervous as a spotty 15 year old who has waited one whole month for his first date. I choose a round of egg and cress sandwiches, which are easy to eat and not too chewy, and a fruit jelly for pudding. I finish off with a frothy coffee, and slide my tray up to the till.

I'm glad I'm still quite steady on my feet as I carry my tray towards Ellen. She even pulls the spare chair out for me as I approach.

"Nice to meet you again, Tom."

"Thought I'd get something to eat today." I plonk my tray on the table and sit down. "How are you?"

I'm so glad to see her, but feel too shy to say her name out loud. This whole situation is preposterous, yet both of us are grinning at each other like those two spotty 15 year olds I just told you about.

"All the better for seeing *you*."

I fumble about trying to open the sandwich box and hope my teeth don't rattle and move about when I have a mouthful of egg. I can tell Ellen has made an effort with her appearance; her hair now looks as though she's had a curly perm, and I notice a trace of eyeshadow and lipstick.

"What have you been doing with yourself since we last met?"

It's a stupid question, but it's all I can think of to ask. I take a bite of the sandwich, and hope I can eat it fast enough before I need to speak again.

"I stayed with my son Bob and his wife for a week or so. They live in Newport, but they also have a house on the mainland that they let out to university students... it's near Cambridge. Term time doesn't start until October, and so it's free for the family to use until then. We went there a couple of weeks ago and they took me out and about.

"Sounds great." I hope I sound enthusiastic enough. "I've been to Cambridge a few times. We did the usual King's College thing, and punting on the Cam. It's all many years ago now."

"Did you go with your wife?"

"Yes." I swallow the last of one of the sandwiches while the recollection of Jean lying back in a punt flashes through my brain. "We'd not long got married. Jean died over a year ago now."

"I'm sorry." Ellen grimaces. "I didn't mean to stoke up old memories. My husband died ten years back, but Bob and Trish have been very kind to me since I've been on my own. They pushed me everywhere around Cambridge in a very comfortable wheelchair. We went to the Corn Exchange Theatre to see a show. Then there were meals out, and shopping in all those little quaint places hidden away down cobblestone alleyways."

"Quite tiring, I expect."

"For *them*, maybe. I was sitting down most of the time. Do you have children?"

"Jean and I were not so fortunate."

"Oh dear, I seem to be asking all the wrong questions today."

I stop short of blurting out that it wasn't through lack of trying. Our favourite pastime throughout the long, dark winter nights of 1963 was attempting to further the Hopkins' dynasty, but our frantic efforts were in vain and all that Jean ended up with was cystitis. By the time my niece got married, I realised parenthood for us would never be on the cards.

"Let's talk about *you* instead. Have you just the one son?"

"Yes. Bob is an only child. He was a GP but took early retirement. Ken and I didn't want any more children, but there were lots of cousins for Bob to play with as I was the youngest of six, and Ken was the middle child of eight. We remembered the noise and arguments. Ken always said it was like living in a nursery."

"That's a good way of putting it." I chuckle and take a sip of tea. "I had a brother, and he only had one daughter. My niece lives in Norfolk. Eddie died a few years back."

"Life can be cruel as we get older, can't it, Tom? Our loved ones die and we're left here with ageing bodies and all we can do is to get on with it."

"Very true." I nod. "Although I hope I'm not done for yet."

"All my siblings are gone, and only a couple of nieces are left on the Island. One grandchild, Stuart, lives abroad, and the other two girls live in London and work all the hours God sends. Ken has two surviving brothers, but they're too old to travel much now."

I start on the jelly, but drop some off the spoon. Should I try and retrieve it? I decide to leave it where it is so I don't show myself up if I make a hash of chasing it around the tray.

"I live in a sheltered housing complex in Bembridge. It's run by the council but we all pay rent. My flat is okay, but I'm the only bloke. The ladies all knock on my door and ask me to fix things."

"I bet they do." Ellen grins. "You should charge them."

"I was a roofer for thirty years. I'm used to mending stuff. The ladies know it too. I wouldn't ask for a penny. I'm okay living on my pensions. Whereabouts do you live?"

"I'm in the BUPA care home in Wroxall, near Appledurcombe House. It's lovely… I have my own room, a hairdresser to do my hair once a week, a podiatrist to cut my toenails, weekly entertainment and exercise classes in the communal lounge, and in fact anything I could ever want. One of the care assistants drove me here today, and she'll pick me up when I ring her. My son and daughter-in-law want me to live with *them*, but I still want my own independence."

It's on the tip of my tongue to ask how much a week this all costs, but hey, it's none of my business.

"Sounds nice. We sold our house and moved into sheltered when Jean became less mobile, but I'm happy enough there."

Yeah, *I* could do with living in a private care home with anything I could ever want, but it sounds a tad expensive. I screw my eyes up to try and read the clock on the wall opposite.

"It's twenty to two." Ellen looks at her watch. "It's been nice meeting you, but I suppose you'd better get to the clinic. After this injection today they said I won't need any more for the time being. Did you see the GP about your eyes?"

"Not yet."

"Don't put it off." Ellen waggles a finger at me. "If it's the same kind of degeneration that I've got, then you'll need injections too so your eyesight doesn't get any worse."

"Yes, Mum."

I smile at her and get to my feet. Due to the fact her course of injections has come to an end, it occurs to me that I'd better not be backward in coming forward.

"See you in the clinic then, and maybe we can meet again?"

"I'd like that. You're more mobile than I am though. There's a get-together lunch at my care home once a fortnight for residents and their friends and family. Come along on Friday to the community hall … Waverley House at Wroxhall, near the Methodist Church. Eleven o'clock. I'll put your name down if you like… it'll be steak pie and veggies this time, we've just had the menu."

"Thank you. That's very kind of you. All I get is toad-in-the-hole. I'll look up the bus times."

I feel like a cat that's got the cream. I feel at ease with Ellen already. I carry my tray to the clearing trolley, grab the stray lump of jelly in one fell swoop, and pop it into my mouth. I look forward to Ellen's turn on the treatment table, as I'm going to make damn sure it's *my* hand holding *hers* this time.

CHAPTER TEN

I've checked the bus timetable at least 10 times, and the journey takes just over an hour; I have to get on the number 8 bus to Sandown at 09:25, and then at Sandown High Street get the number 3 at 09:40 to Wroxall Methodist Church. I don't care about the journey home, but I want to arrive on time. Actually, I'm going to be about 45 minutes early, but as my old dad used to say…rather early than late.

I cut myself shaving this morning, and now there's a mark on my cheek. I don't know what to wear, but I guess nobody will be looking at *me*. I choose a nice beige top that Jean bought me for my 80th birthday, and put on a clean pair of trousers. The doorbell rings just as I'm trying to lace up my shoes without taking the easy option of sliding into the Velcro ones. My heart sinks at the sight of Cissie Thompson.

"Hello Cissie, I'm just about to catch the bus."

"Tom, my toaster's up the spout. I told you about it ages ago. Remember?

"Sorry, I forgot. Well… I can't do anything at the moment. I'll have a look at it when I get back."

"Where are you going?"

Cissie is a nosey old biddy. If I tell her I'm meeting a lady friend, it'll be all around the complex in five minutes flat.

"To Newport."

Cissie turns away and I breathe a sigh of relief. I grab my wallet and blazer, and hope I'm presentable enough for the residents of Waverley House.

I'm there at Steyne Park with about ten minutes to wait until the bus to Sandown arrives. I didn't have time to pop in and say good morning to Jean, and now I feel guilty as I climb on the bus and then doubly guilt-ridden as I think about meeting up with Ellen. It's another nice autumn morning and the bus trundles away to Sandown with only a few elderly passengers on board. None of us have paid any fare by the looks of it, and I wonder how the heck Southern Vectis can make a profit.

I arrive at Wroxall at 10:30, make a quick reccy as to the whereabouts of Waverley House, and then decide to sit in the church until 10:50 in the hope that the vicar doesn't appear and try to save my soul. In a kind of excited nervous state, I knock on Waverley's main door right on time and come face to face with a plump, motherly middle-aged woman in a nurse's uniform.

"I'm Tom Hopkins. I'm here to see Ellen Wilkinson. She invited me to the lunch for friends and family."

"I'm Sister Wraight. Come in for a moment. There might be a problem with that, but I'll get Ellen for you and she can explain."

"There's no problem, I'm sure. Ellen invited me and I'm here at her request. She said she put my name down for the lunch."

Sister Wraight ushers me in to a plush hallway with wall lights that remind me of Olympic torches. Background music seems to be coming out of the plant pots lined up on either side, which house ferns of various sizes. The Persian rug feels soft under my feet. I sit on a nearby chair and wait, with my heart beating faster in anticipation.

After a few minutes Ellen comes towards me, leaning on a walker. I stand up and smile at her.

"Thanks again for inviting me. It's a lovely place. I can see why you like it here."

"Sorry, Tom, but I didn't have your phone number. Bob and Trish have turned up, and residents are only allowed two guests for lunch to make sure there's enough food to go around."

Disappointment doesn't cover it… no… I'm *angry*. I've been looking forward to this moment all week. I've even missed my Tesco run with Doreen, and now I haven't got any lunch to eat and have to get back on the bus.

"But you invited me…" My voice rises a couple of tones. "Did your son know I was coming?"

"Yes, I told him on Wednesday, but they arrived this morning for an unexpected visit and so how could I turn them away?"

At the end of the hallway I notice a rather stout and florid man striding with some purpose towards us. Straight away I know by some other-worldly intuition that this is Bob, who by the looks of him definitely does *not* need to eat my steak pie. In fact I don't think he needs to eat anything at all for a whole month.

"Ah, there you are, Mum." Bob ignores me completely. "We wondered where you'd got to."

"I'm talking to my friend. Bob, this is Tom who I told you about. He does voluntary work at the hospital."

I want to kick Bob in the balls, but tear my gaze away from Ellen and force my mouth into something approaching a smile.

"Pleased to meet you, Bob."

Bob looks as though he wants to stab me through the heart. If I had a gun I'd shoot the bastard. Bob gives a brief nod of acknowledgement.

"Likewise, I'm sure."

"Sorry Tom, but you see I'm not allowed three extra people for lunch. If I did, then everyone would do it and then they'd be short of food."

"Is there a café nearby where I can eat? After lunch I can come back if you like."

"I'm afraid that's not possible today. Trish and I are taking Mum out for the afternoon."

I'm not one to be trumped. BB…Bastard Bob… might have got there first, but *I'm* going to have the last say.

"Give me your phone number, Ellen. I'll call and we can arrange to meet another day."

"That will be lovely."

There's virtual steam coming out of BB's ears. I see a 'Waverley House' notepad on the hall table. I tear off the top sheet of paper and reach in my blazer for a pen. After Ellen gives me her number I hold the paper triumphantly aloft.

"Expect a phone call very soon."

"Great, and I'm sorry again for today."

I ignore Bob, say my farewells to Ellen, and reluctantly turn on my heel and head off in the direction of the bus stop.

***

I give Bastard Bob and his wife enough time to take their leave, and dial Ellen's number later that evening. It rings a few times but then I hear her voice.

"Hello."

"Hi, Ellen. It's Tom. Has your son gone home?"

"Yes. I wondered if you would call today."

"Where did they take you this afternoon?"

"Oh …nowhere after all. We sat in the garden."

I make an involuntary fist with my free hand, and decide on the spot that next time nobody is going to stop me visiting my new friend.

"I'm happy to come along to the next lunch if you like?"

"Lovely… yes. That will be the week after next on the Friday."

"What about your son and his wife?" I don't even want to say the bloke's name.

"I won't tell them you're coming. How about that?"

"Sounds good to me." I break into a grin. "Can you see my number on your phone? Write it down and call any time you like."

"Yes, I can see it. Will do. Bye for now, Tom. There's a sing-song in the hall that I've got to go to now."

"Enjoy yourself. See you soon."

I replace the receiver with a sigh. Now I've got to wait another two weeks. All I can hope for is that Bob doesn't get wind of our plans and decides to wreck them again. For as far as I can tell, Bob aims to swat any bee who has the temerity to buzz around his mother. Let me tell you, I'm after no pot of honey. It's just enough for me to have found a friend. At my age when all your loved ones are six foot under, you need all the friends you can get.

CHAPTER ELEVEN

Everything looks pink, and I've got a headache from the optician's bright light which has shone in the back of my eyes for the last ten minutes, not to mention wanting to gag from his halitosis.

"The dye will wear off very soon, Mr Hopkins. I'm going to refer you to the eye clinic at St. Jude's for them to keep a check on you. I've done all the tests, and you have early stage dry age-related macular degeneration. There's no cure, but you don't need treatment yet. Do you know St. Jude's?

"Whoop de doo dah. Isn't life grand?" I blink a few times and the pinkness starts to fade. "Ironically, I work in the eye clinic itself."

"Really?"

The optician glances at my notes to obviously make a surreptitious check of my age.

"Voluntary work."

"Well, you'll know all about AMD then."

"I'm learning."

"Eat well and help yourself … plenty of brightly coloured vegetables to get your vitamins."

"Thank you." I stand up. "I guess I've just got to live with it."

"I'm afraid so. If it progresses to the wet type, then the hospital can give you some treatment."

I step out into a cold, grey afternoon that matches my mood. Getting old is not for the faint-hearted. What with the achy joints, reduced income and Jean's death, I've now got dodgy eyes as well. I kick a can into the gutter and muse over Mum's words all those years ago that life goes tits up from about the age of about seventy five. I think she was right, but hey, I'm down but not out. I can still walk home from Bembridge High Street, and so I do.

***

The phone rings as I turn the key in the lock. It's a little boost to my overall melancholia to hear Ellen's voice on the other end.

"Hello Tom. How are you today?"

"Oh… so-so."

"You sound depressed."

"Just been diagnosed with dry AMD."

"Well, that's not as bad as I've got, so you're better off than me."

"I'd dance around the room if I could."

"Cheer up, it's only forever."

I have a little chuckle at her words, and blurt out the first thing that comes into my head.

"Why don't you get one of your care workers to drive you over here for a visit? We could have a chat and some lunch and set the world to rights."

"I'd like that. They always want to earn more money. I can't get on and off the buses any more."

"That's settled then. What day can they bring you?"

"I don't know yet, Tom. I'd have to ask and book it up. There's a procedure for that sort of thing. I'd have to let you know."

"Okay. I can always re-arrange my brain surgery."

"D'you think that's wise?"

I can hear Ellen's high pitched laugh on the other end of the line. I like a woman with a sense of humour – life's too grim without it.

It's only a short while later that the phone rings for the second time today. As I hardly have any callers I can only assume that it's Ellen again, but I don't recognise the number on the screen. I pick up the receiver.

"Okay, I've had my brain surgery. You can come over now."

"I'm afraid that won't be possible."

I'm slightly flummoxed to hear a male voice on the other end of the line.

"Who is this please?"

"This is Robert Wilkinson. My mother is not well enough to travel outside of the home other than to go to the hospital for her appointments."

"Are you keeping her prisoner then?" My hand grips the receiver with more force. "She seemed quite all right the last time I saw her."

"She is elderly and needs to be looked after. As her son, this duty falls to *myself* to carry out."

"Look, mate. All I'm doing is inviting her for lunch. She's going to book a ride there and back from one of the care workers."

"I'm not your mate, and I'll thank you to leave my mother alone."

The line goes dead. I'm fuming. I pace the small confines of my living room a few times and then pick up the receiver again and dial Ellen's number.

"Hello?"

"Ellen, this is Tom again."

"Oh, hi Tom. Anything wrong?"

"Well… yes. I've just had a phone call from your son, who has warned me off seeing you. I thought you weren't going to tell him that you were coming to my flat for lunch."

"I didn't, truly I didn't. I'm sorry if Bob has upset you."

"Who did you tell? It's weird…like he doesn't want you to go anywhere or see anyone."

"I filled in a travel form to book a ride. That's all I did."

"Ellen… someone in the home must have told Bob straight away. What I need to do then is to arrive at your place with no warning and when you know Bob won't be there."

"If you don't want to go to the lunch, then you can come any day after half past two. We have our meal at mid-day, and then it's quiet time for a couple of hours. Visitors can come between half past two and five o'clock."

"Right, I'll do that. What day would you like me to visit? Tomorrow?"

"Yes, tomorrow then. I won't say a word to anybody."

"Open the main door at three o'clock, and I'll be standing there. I won't knock."

"Right you are. I look forward to it."

I end the call and stand deep in thought. Something about Bob's behaviour doesn't sit right with me. Apart from my father who has long been in his grave, I've never let anybody dictate to me what I can or cannot do. I left home at seventeen to get away from Hopkins Senior, and even at my advanced age I am not about to kowtow to *anybody*, especially Bob Wilkinson. I will see my new friend Ellen with or without his permission.

I think of all the ways I could kill Bob while I prepare my evening meal. Shooting him is too easy… he would need to suffer a bit first. If I were fifty years younger I could string the fat bastard up by his feet and let him hang over a precipice somewhere. He'd beg for mercy, but I'd cut the string and watch him drop.

Sausages cooking in the fat from my breakfast bacon (sorry Jean) sizzle and spit in the pan. I turn them onto a pink side and imagine pouring boiling oil down Bob's throat. The man brings out my most violent side, but don't think too badly of me… I'm usually quite a calm and peace-loving bloke; really I am. It's just that at my age I don't want to be controlled by *anybody*, and I'm sure *you* wouldn't want to be either, would you?

CHAPTER TWELVE

Will she remember? As I approach the main door of Ellen's care home the church clock strikes the hour. I can hear some activity on the other side, and presently Ellen pulls the door ajar. I grin at her.

"Hey! We meet again!"

"Come in, come in." Ellen holds the door open wider. "It's all very quiet here… I think everyone's still asleep."

There are no members of staff about. Ellen, both hands clutching her walker, leads me along a carpeted passageway with grab rails on both sides. She stops outside number 3, which boasts a freshly painted front door, and unlocks it with a key.

"This is my flat, and there's just *me* living here. As I said before, Hubby died ten years ago."

I walk into the past as soon as I step over the threshold. What looks like an expensive antique polished sideboard graces the hallway. Sepia photographs hang from a picture rail, and a large aspidistra in an iron pot stands next to the sideboard.

"Wow… I love the sideboard."

"Well… thank you. My husband was an antiques dealer. You'll not find anything modern in this flat."

I walk into the living room and catch my breath. The windows are framed by thick green velvet curtains held back with tassels. Two ornate rosewood cabinets complete with trailing vine carvings are filled with crystal and china and sit either side of an open fireplace stuffed with decorative logs. In front of the fireplace is one of those old type Victorian screens. The sofa and armchairs are of the same green velvet as the curtains, and edged with rosewood and with similar trailing vine carvings as the cabinets. A grandfather clock ticks away in one corner next to a Steinway piano. In front of the sofa is a small mahogany coffee table which looks solid and is edged with gold leaf. The carpet is obviously Persian and fills the entire floor. There's serious money here, and I suddenly feel out of my depth. It has occurred to me in an instant why Bastard Bob might be getting a little edgy.

"Good God…what a beautiful room! I feel like I'm back in eighteen ninety. Queen Victoria would feel at home here."

"She would, wouldn't she? I blame Ken for that. I had to sell the claw bath when I moved here though…I couldn't get in and out of it anymore and now have to use a walk in shower." Ellen chuckles and eases herself down onto an armchair. "Anyway, sit yourself down. I've ordered an afternoon tea for us both. One of the girls will bring it along in a short while."

Seated in the other armchair, I cannot stop gazing about the place, and try not to feel ashamed of my sparse, well-worn furniture which has stood Jean and me in good stead over many years. However, since I've been a pensioner it has never occurred to me to splash out money unnecessarily on anything new. I take another glance at the Steinway with its matching green velvet stool and sheets of music on the shelf above the keyboard.

"Do you play the piano?"

"I do indeed." Ellen nods. "Mostly by memory now, as the eyes aren't that good for reading little crotchets and quavers."

"Could you play something for me?"

"Oh… yes, I can if you really want me to. What would you like me to play?"

"I'm not too hot on the classical stuff. My mum used to sing *I'll Take You Home Again, Kathleen*."

"Yes, I know that one." Ellen stands up and makes her way to the piano. "I remember all the old songs."

I'm seven years old and back in my mother's kitchen as Ellen starts to play. We're snuggled on the sofa next to the old range cooker; my brother on one side of Mum, and me on the other. Mum has her arms around both of us and is singing about somebody called Kathleen. Who she is and why she can't make her own way home I've no idea, but it's a nice tune.

"Penny for your thoughts. You look miles away."

I open my eyes and shoot back to reality in an instant. I'm a stupid old man who has let his mind wander back too many years. I hadn't even realised the song had come to an end.

"You're very talented. For a moment I was back home and it was the end of World War Two."

"Ken used to like me to play Chopin."

I realise with some surprise that Ellen is quite a cultured lady. I'm about to ask her for another song when there's a knock on the door. A member of staff then lets herself in, gives Ellen a smile, and pushes a laden trolley towards the coffee table.

"Afternoon tea, as Madam ordered."

"Thanks Susan." Ellen turns around on the piano stool. "This is my new friend Tom."

"Hello Tom."

"Hi."

I stand up. Susan gives me a quick glance and then transfers a teapot, crockery and a selection of cakes to the table.

"I'll leave the two of you now to enjoy your tea."

I'm relieved that Susan hasn't asked me to go home, and in a way triumphant that Bob is still ignorant of the fact that his mother and I are sitting quite comfortably in her living room. I help myself to a cream cake, and content, I relax a bit more.

"We'll have to do this more often."

"I agree." Ellen chooses a piece of lemon sponge. "It's good to have visitors. Bob always plays up like a spoilt child if I have friends in."

"He doesn't need to know, does he?" I take a delicious bite of cake. "It'll be our little secret."

We talk about this and that… nothing at all of any importance. An hour or so later after the cake plate, teapot and cups are empty, I hear the front door open and presume Susan has let herself in again. I make a neat pile of used crockery on the tray, then pick the tray up, get to my feet, and turn towards the door. However, I don't like what I see, especially when the shouting starts.

"What are *you* doing here?"

It's Bastard Bob, whose crimson features have contorted into an expression of seemingly murderous intent. I place the tray down carefully on the table.

"Your mother invited me. We were having a nice time until *you* turned up."

I may be an old boy, but Bastard Bob is not going to get the better of me. Hey, I'm committing no crime … just having a chat with a new friend. This bloke is beginning to get on my tits.

"Bob, I don't know what your problem is, but you need to mind your own business. Ellen and I are friends, and it's got nothing to do with *you*."

"It's got *everything* to do with me. I look after her, and she shouldn't have too many visitors."

Ellen isn't backing me up for some unknown reason. Bob towers over me and for a split second I consider ramming one of the cake knives into his eye. I take a couple of steps backwards and place myself on the other side of the table.

"Bob, I'm going to sit back down. You can either join us, or you can piss off."

I turn away and walk with some purpose towards the armchair. I'm quite relieved to take the weight off my legs, as I suddenly feel as though they don't belong to me. I look at Ellen, who gives the impression of wanting to be somewhere else. Bob is breathing hard, like an old dray horse that has dragged its load up a hill. To my astonishment he then makes for the door and slams it on his way out.

"What's his problem?" I shake my head in disbelief. "We're just sitting here having a chat."

"I'm sorry, Tom. I think it's best that you go."

There's something odd going on here. Ellen wrings her hands and seems near to tears. I stick my neck out and hope for the best.

"Are you frightened of him?"

"No of course not. He's always had a quick temper. Please go, then he'll calm down and we'll be back to normal. If you don't leave, then he'll be back with the manager and the security guy."

"So he's done this before then?"

"Please… Tom…"

Ellen glances at the door, as though she expects it to burst open at any moment. I have an idea, but first I have to remember my manners.

"Thank you very much for the tea and your company. I'll phone you when I get home and make sure you're all right."

Our little afternoon meeting has gone sour, thanks again to Bob. I stand up and give Ellen my best smile, which is not reciprocated. Time to go on my way… for the moment anyway.

The corridor outside Ellen's flat is empty. I follow the sound of rattling crockery to where Susan loads a dishwasher in the main kitchen area.

"Oh, hello Tom. Can I help you?"

"Yes… er… this is a bit awkward. I was wondering whether you'd told Bob Wilkinson that I was visiting his mother."

Susan's face flushes as red as a beetroot, which kind of gives the game away.

"Sorry… some time ago he asked all the carers to let him know when Ellen has visitors. If *I* hadn't done it then somebody else would have phoned him."

My blood is boiling. I'm stymied for today. I need to catch the bus home and think about my next move, as despite Bob's actions I don't intend to give up my new-found friendship so easily.

As soon as I reach my flat I ring Ellen's number. There's quite a wait before she answers.

"Hello?"

"Ellen… it's Tom. Are you on your own?"

"No."

"Okay. Just to let you know I'm home and that we can meet up again any time you like. Yes? No?"

"Yes."

"Great. We'll find a way around this. Ring me when you're on your own."

I end the call and feel a small shiver of triumph run up my spine.

CHAPTER THIRTEEN

"You're quiet today, Tom."

We're in-between patients, and Miss Rose has obviously said something to me but for the life of me I can't remember what it was. Before I have a chance to answer I hear the nurse call in the last one on the list. It's a chap about my own age who gives me that familiar *why is that old man still working* look before he's invited to lie down on the treatment couch. His gnarled fist is putty in my hand as the needle makes its way towards his eye.

"Soon be over."

I stare at the clinic door until Miss Rose finishes, and imagine how Ellen might never walk in here again. Somehow volunteering at the hospital isn't giving me the same pleasure now as it had before. I've even taken to catching the latest bus possible and eating lunch before I leave. I haven't heard from Ellen in three weeks, and to be honest… I miss her.

The man thanks me and hurries off as fast as he can. Miss Rose whips off her plastic gloves.

"Come on Tom, there's something wrong, isn't there?"

"Oh, just a tricky little hiccup, but I'll sort something out."

"Well, if you like, we can sort it out together."

"That's very kind of you, but you don't want to be bothered with my problems."

"Tom, if you don't tell me what's wrong, then how can I help you?"

I feel rather foolish to be honest; a man my age shouldn't have lady troubles. I take a deep breath.

"It's very kind of you, Miss Rose…"

"Call me Sara, and start again."

"It's very kind of you, Sara, to want to listen. In a nutshell, I made a friend of one of the patients here, and now her son is trying to stop us seeing each other. She doesn't need any more treatment, and so she won't be back. The staff at her care home tell the son straight away if she has a visitor. I think he might have even cut off her phone, because I tried to ring her this morning and just got a discontinued sound. We don't have mobiles… I can't get my head around them."

"Well, he can't do that, Tom, and you know it. I'm a sucker for romance, and so what I'll do is send her a late check-up appointment. You can meet her here after clinic finishes."

"She's Mister Joe's patient."

"So, I'll speak to Joe and sort it for you. He owes me a favour anyway. If you give me your number I'll phone you and let you know the time and date. I'll overbook her onto one of my afternoon clinics."

"I don't know what to say…thanks so much, Sara." I scribble my number down and hand it to her. "You're very kind. Hopefully he'll drop her off and go and get a cup of tea or something."

"If he tries to come into the room I'll say it's stated in her notes that she does not want anybody to accompany her. I'll say it in my best doctor voice. You've helped a lot of people here, Tom, and so now it's *your* turn."

I'm not usually one for tearing up and blubbing, and so now I'm embarrassed in case Sara sees my watery eyes. I turn away and tidy some shelves for something to do.

***

True to her word, Sara phones me a couple of days later with the news that Ellen's appointment will be after clinic at 4:30pm in a week's time. It's a long wait, but I manage to occupy myself doing some more line dancing, weeding the communal garden, and raking up mountains of leaves. I even mended Cissie's toaster. I've given up Bingo though, and to be honest, I'm relieved about that. When Sara's clinic comes around again I have my lunch before I go, so that I don't see Bastard Bob if he's in the café.

It's a long two and a half hours before Ellen's appointment, and when the last patient leaves I wash my hands and straighten my tie.

"Tom, I'll get the nurse to call your friend in now, and I'll make sure nobody else follows her in. I'll see you next time."

"Thank you so much, Sara. I'm very grateful."

I'm left alone in the treatment room, and I stare at the door. Presently Ellen walks in and appears somewhat depressed. However, her eyes light up when she catches sight of me.

"Tom! I'm so glad to see you!"

"How are you?" I walk towards her. "I asked Miss Rose to send you an appointment. I was worried that I couldn't get in touch with you."

"What's the matter with my eyes? I thought I'd had all my injections."

"You have." I nod. "Miss Rose organised this for us so that we could meet. I wondered why I couldn't get you on the phone."

I'm surprised when Ellen's bright expression crumbles and her eyes fill with tears.

"Tom…I lied…Bob isn't as nice as I first made out. He's not letting me see anyone or speak to anyone. I'm being held a virtual prisoner in my own home. He's got the staff watching every move I make. He's probably told them I'm doo-lally or something."

"It's because of *me*, isn't it?" My right hand makes an involuntary fist. "Where is he now?"

"Upstairs in the café, I expect. The doctor told him I didn't need a chaperone and to go and get a cup of coffee."

"Let's get a taxi to my place. There's an empty guest suite where you can stay. He doesn't know where I live. You can stay with me for as long as you like."

"I can't do that!" Ellen looks aghast. "He'll have the police out searching the country! Anyway, I've got no other clothes with me."

"So what? The warden has a cupboard full of clothes, don't ask where they're from, and anyway, we can always buy some. Let's go *now*. A cup of coffee won't last very long. If you give me the number of your home, I'll phone your matron from the phone in this room and tell her you're okay, but I won't let her know where you're staying. Hopefully they'll be too busy to answer and I can just leave a message."

I can see by her expression that she's considering my offer. I don't know what's made me blurt out such a thing, but for the first time in my life I've taken a risk and it feels *good*. After a few agonising minutes Ellen wipes her eyes and smiles at me as she takes what looks like a small diary out of her shoulder bag.

"Okay. I'm a grown woman. The number's on the front page of this address book. I shouldn't have to live like this. I'll let you into a little secret…I haven't made a will yet, and Bob thinks you're after my money."

"Ellen, I wouldn't touch a penny." I take the book from her and open the cover. "He's got it all wrong. I just want to be your friend."

"I know. I know. He's at me night and day to see a solicitor to draw up a will, but I'm a stubborn old woman. I'll give my money to whoever I want to."

I pick up a phone extension on the wall, dial 9 for an outside line, then tap in the number on the front page. It rings several times before an answerphone kicks in. I have a quick change of mind while the message plays and hand the receiver to Ellen.

"Say you're okay and staying with a friend." I whisper as softly as I can. "But don't say with whom or where."

I'm sweating with relief as she leaves a short message and then replaces the receiver. I move past her.

"Come on… we've got to go."

I make my way to the door and look from left to right. The coast is empty, and the main entrance is only a short walk from Outpatients. I've often seen taxis waiting in laybys out the front of the hospital on the off-chance, and so hopefully we'll be in luck. I beckon to Ellen to follow me, but with her needing a walker I know we're not going to be able to move very fast.

"Quick as you can, before he comes back."

We giggle and move at our normal snail's pace along the corridor. A couple of nurses smile at us as we exit Outpatients, as though they know exactly what we're doing. We skirt around people milling about at the main entrance, and I signal to rather bored- looking taxi driver in his vehicle who sits in a layby next to a 'No Waiting' notice. He perks up and starts his engine. I walk over to him and he winds down his window.

"Where to, mate?"

"Steyne Road, Bembridge, by the Co-op. There's two of us." I'm careful not to give my address. I beckon Ellen forward and open the back door of the taxi. "My friend has a walking frame. Can you put it somewhere, please?"

The driver gets out, helps Ellen into the taxi, and stows the walker in the boot. I let out a huge sigh as the taxi pulls away.

"There'll be a little bit of a trek when we get out, but not too far."

"Tom, I don't know if I've done the right thing." Ellen shakes her head. "Bob will cause such a fuss."

"You left a message at your place. They'll hear your voice and assume you're okay. He's got no right to keep you prisoner."

I don't know for certain how the staff will react, but I'm riding high and pleased as punch to have Ellen with me, even for a few short days.

"Are the clothes from dead people?"

"Probably. The relatives leave them." I look at Ellen and laugh. "But they're very clean. Warden Penny would have put them through the boil wash first."

"Even the knickers?"

I don't want to think about dead people's knickers, or the sight of Ellen wearing them. To be honest it just doesn't seem right.

"The Co-op where we're going will have some you can buy, I'm sure."

I try and think of a different subject other than Ellen's knickers. I can see a smirk on the taxi driver's face.

CHAPTER FOURTEEN

I did not expect Bob would react so quickly to his mother's disappearance, and so I'm a bit shocked to see Ellen's face appear on the 'Look South' TV programme two days' later as we finish our dinner.

"Tom… that's me!" Ellen pauses in mid-chew and stares at the screen. "What are we going to do?"

"Just stay here in the guest suite for now. I don't think anybody's clocked you. I'll think of something."

I stop talking, as I can't think and speak at the same time. Ellen apparently also has difficulty in doing this, because she blurts out something that makes me sit up straighter and wonder if she's given any thought to her words at all.

"We can get married."

"What?" I look at her, aghast. The woman has lost her marbles for sure.

"It will work, trust me. Once we're married, then you'll be my next of kin. I'll make a will in your favour and Bob will have to whistle."

I give a roar of laughter at the mental image of me trying to get a wedding ring past Ellen's arthritic knuckle.

"That's a good one. We hardly know each other."

"So… it'll be a marriage of convenience. Bob will then leave me alone, and you'll have the convenience of all my money and the choice of who to give it to when I'm gone and you've got one foot in the grave."

"You're younger than me. I've already *got* one foot in the grave."

"Then you'd better not take too much time to think about what you're going to do with it. I've known for ages that Bob is just after my money, and I'll go satisfied into the next world with the knowledge that he hasn't ended up with any."

"What about your grandchildren?"

"What about them?" Ellen shrugs. "I never see them and they haven't contacted me in ages. They'll soon pop up to see what they can grab when I'm dead though, and so *they're* not getting my money either."

To say I'm flabbergasted would be an understatement. The whole situation is preposterous. Ellen is deadly serious, but the more I think about what she has said the more I might be able to twist it around to make some kind of sense. I don't really want to know how much money she has, but to get married would put a stop to Bob's harassment of her. He would have to sit on his middle finger and cry.

"Ellen, I don't want your money."

"Well, if we're married then you're getting it. You're a good man, and hopefully we've got a few years left between us to enjoy it and have a round the world cruise or something. But… no sex though, and separate cabins. I'm past all that and need to get that out in the open to start with. I just want us to be friends. We can be great company for each other."

As my old dad used to say… I don't know whether to have a shit or a haircut. I'm a lonely old widower who holds hands with people for something to do, and it was only a short time ago that I'd sat at this table with Jean, the woman I'd loved since I was a young man and who I thought would outlive me. A round-the-world cruise sounds out of my league, let alone getting a marriage proposal at my advanced age.

"This is crazy. We can't just go and get married."

"Yes we can, at St.Catherine's Ceremony Room at Newport. One of my carers did, and she didn't have to wait very long to do it, either. She booked it with the council. What do you say? Yes or no?"

I don't really know what to say. I'm used to my sedate and comfortable life here in Bembridge at the sheltered housing complex. Mondays and Thursdays every week I go to the eye clinic, Tuesdays is Bingo and Wednesdays is line dancing. Fridays is Tesco shopping, and Saturdays I go to Newport. What the hell do I know about round-the-world cruises? But hey, most likely I'll be dead in what… two years? Five years?

"Yes."

I can't believe I just said that. Ellen's face lights up and she puts down her knife and fork.

"You won't regret this, Tom. We can have a great life for whatever time we've got left. There's more to life than just sex you know."

If I'd been sixty years younger I might have disagreed with her last statement. Anyway…should I kiss the bride-to-be? Would that be un-gentlemanly seeing as all Ellen wants is a platonic relationship? I'm not sure the old chap could ever rise to the occasion now anyway. As a man though, I feel I have to make a move of some kind.

"Would you like a kiss to celebrate?"

"Oh, no, we don't have to do that." Ellen actually blushes as she shakes her head. "You're my friend, and we've both had previous partners when we were younger for *that* kind of thing."

To be honest, it's a relief, as I couldn't ever think about kissing any other woman except Jean. I'm glad the '*that*-kind-of thing' is out of the way. We can enjoy each other's company and get one over on Bastard Bob.

Ah, Bastard Bob… the elephant in the room. He's here with us even though we're loathe to mention him. I'm not keen on being in the same room as Bob when he finds out I've married his mother.

"Look… it's going to be a bit awkward when Bob hears the news." I pop the last potato into my mouth. "Are you going to tell him?"

"Only after we're married. You'll be able to move in to my flat if you like. There are two bedrooms."

"I don't think that's the best idea, seeing as Bob already has the staff watching you there."

"Ah yes, you're right, Tom. I'll stay here then, until we can buy a bungalow somewhere."

"I don't think I can stretch to half." I suddenly feel like one of those old gigolos.

"No, this is my idea and I've got more than enough money. Don't you worry about *anything*."

Any other bloke would be cock-a-hoop at hearing this. I feel a bit uneasy to tell you the truth, because this will only reinforce Bob's opinion that I'm a gold-digger. This has all landed in my lap, so to speak. It's a nice thing to happen to me, but I didn't ask for it.

"I like to pay my way. I want to help out with the bills. Unless I can contribute then we'll have to stay where we are."

"Oh, well in that case I accept your offer." Ellen gives me a smile. "We'll work it out, Tom."

I'm sure we will, but in the meantime Bob has reported Ellen as a missing person, and sooner or later the police will be kicking my door in. Something has to be done.

"Ellen, you'll need to speak to the police and say that you're okay and are staying with a friend. They'll then know you're of sound mind. You'll have to convince them that Bob has over-reacted. We'll have to go out and use a public phone box, otherwise they might trace the call straight back here. I'll get one of Jean's hats… see if we can disguise your features a bit."

"Have I got to go? There's a way of withholding a number, I'm sure."

"There probably is, but I don't know it. Hey, I've still got Jean's wheelchair in storage. I'll get it and then we can go along to the supermarket, where there's a phone outside we can use. I've written down a number for the police in my diary. Just say that you don't want Bob to know where you are."

"I *don't* want him to know where I am."

"Then you're not telling lies, are you?"

I know she's not keen to go out, but needs must. The police have to stop the search, and the sooner they do that the easier I'll rest in my bed tonight.

***

I don't think I'm as fit as I used to be. Ellen's only a lightweight but it's not easy pushing her along in a wheelchair, especially when going up or down a kerb. I'm puffing a bit as we reach the phone box. I never used to have this much trouble with Jean, but back then I was a few years younger.

"Come on, I'll help you out…oh, wait a minute."

I open the door to the phone box, which has now turned into a defibrillator station instead. My heart sinks to my boots. It'll be a long walk back to the flat. I should have remembered nobody uses public phones anymore. Looks like Ellen will have to use my landline after all. The police will track the call faster than I can say *Bastard Bob.*

***

The policewoman is very kind, but I'm uneasy and hope that Ellen can convince her that we're not a pair of raving lunatics.

"So… Mrs Wilkinson… why did your son think you had gone missing?"

"I've no idea." Ellen smiles at the policewoman. "All I'm doing is staying here with my friend. I didn't tell my son because I'm a grown woman with my own life, and I didn't want him to know where I am."

"I see." The policeman gives a sage nod as though part of a conspiracy. "You caused him some worry though."

"He's a big boy now. He'll get over it. I take it my secret is safe with you?"

"Of course. I'll tell him you're okay, but I won't give your location away."

"Thank you." Ellen looks as though butter wouldn't melt in her mouth. "I'm much obliged."

We both give a heartfelt sigh when I return to the front room after showing the policewoman out.

"Thank God for that." I sink down into an armchair.

"Do you think she was convinced, Tom?"

"I hope so. Anyway, we haven't done anything wrong."

"Tom… Bob's going to be angry when he finds out what's been going on, and so we'll need to get away very soon after the wedding to give him time to cool off. Can we go along to the council offices tomorrow and book it?"

"Yes, we'll get a taxi. It's an eye clinic day though, but I'm only a volunteer, and so it's up to me whether or not I work. I'll have to give them a call in the morning though and let them know I won't be in."

I don't want to think about what Bob's going to do. More to the point it's the first eye clinic I would have missed since I started volunteering at the hospital. Still, what's more important than arranging my own wedding? What would *you* do?

***

I'm disappointed to hear Sara's voice on the other end of the line. She's the last person I wanted to pick up the phone. I would have rather spoken to Mister Joe. I take a deep breath.

"Sara, this is Tom. You know… the volunteer."

"Hi Tom the volunteer. How are you?"

"I'm fine. I'm just letting you know that I won't be in today."

"You're not well?"

"I am well. It's just …"

"Yes?"

"It's just that…I'm going to get married again and we need to go to Newport today to book the wedding."

"That's fantastic!" Sara sounds genuinely thrilled. "Is it the lady I arranged for you to meet after clinic recently?"

"Yes. It's all happened so quickly, but hey, we're not getting any younger."

"Tom, you go and get your wedding sorted out. We can cope. Don't worry about *us*… just concentrate on yourself."

After I say goodbye and replace the receiver I feel a bit of a heel for letting them all down. Some of the patients need a hand to hold, but then again… so do I.

CHAPTER FIFTEEN

"The marriage is for yourselves?"

The administrator tries hard not to show her surprise, but she doesn't quite manage it. I realise we're not love's young dream anymore, but hey, we're still people and so why shouldn't we get married if we want to?

"Yes."

We both speak at the same time. The woman's features break out into a grin.

"Well, I think that's wonderful!"

Perhaps she'll give us the service free out of the goodness of her heart then? After all, we're so old we might not even make it to the wedding day.

"It just so happens I had a cancellation yesterday. I can get you in for Friday next week."

I think of the poor young bride-to-be or groom who must be devastated after their partner had a change of heart. The caterers had no doubt been booked, and the happy couple's faces were already on the tea towels so to speak. But hey, one door closes and another one opens so they say. However, it's taking shape for *us* rather sooner than I'd bargained for. Suddenly it all doesn't seem real; it should be *Jean* sitting here with me. But in the back of my mind I know Jean still lies under the ground, dead as a bloody dodo.

"That will be marvellous." Ellen claps her hands with joy. "Friday it is, then. There will just be ourselves with two witnesses."

"As you please." The administrator taps something into a computer. "We'll go over some more details, and I'll need proof of your names, dates of birth and addresses, but you will be able to arrive at St. Catherine's Ceremony Room next Friday at half past ten."

***

I feel somewhat dazed as we exit the council offices. I look around for Bob, but so far so good. By the end of next week I'll have a new wife, and we'll be getting ready for a round-the-world cruise if Ellen has anything to do with it.

"I want to get a will sorted out now. I've left it too long." From her wheelchair Ellen looks up and turns towards me over her shoulder. "Pearce, Legg and Wayburn next to W.H Smith's is the one Ken used to use. We've got time for lunch first."

"Whatever you want. We've got the taxi all day."

The driver has fallen asleep in the car park. I tap lightly on the window and he sits up, yawns, and opens his door.

"Sorry to disturb you. Please can you drop us off at the end of the High Street and then come back for us outside Smith's at four o'clock."

"Will do, mate."

After a short ride we get out of the taxi again. I decide to wheel Ellen along to my favourite café.

"What do you say to the Blue Door for lunch? I go there most Saturdays."

"It sounds charming." Ellen's head with Jean's hat on it nods up and down. "I'm sure anywhere you go is fine with me."

Diane is on duty again as I push the café door open and then manoeuvre Ellen inside.

"Hello again, Tom." Diane runs around to hold open the door. "Is it Saturday again already?"

"No, only Thursday." I laugh in reply. "Any free tables?"

"Yes, go on in, and there's two left. Is this your friend?"

"Yes, I'm Ellen." Ellen holds out one hand to Diane. "Tom's told me all about this place."

"Pleased to meet you." Diane shakes Ellen's hand. "Same as usual for you, Tom?"

"No, I think I'll have a look at the menu and choose something else. My life's going to change very soon, and so it's time for a different lunch."

"Really? Make yourselves comfortable and then you can tell me all about it."

I push Ellen towards a table, help her transfer to a seat, and then fold the wheelchair so it's out of the way. I feel very brave when deciding on a prawn baguette instead of the ham omelette. Diane heads towards our table with a small notebook in one hand.

"Don't keep me in suspense, Tom. What's happening with you?"

"We're getting married." Ellen waves her menu in the air. "And I'll go for a jacket potato with cheese, please."

"Really? Married? Congratulations!"

"Thanks, Diane. Prawn baguette for me please."

I still can't believe I'll soon have a new wife. Diane looks as bewildered as I surely do, although after the initial shock she does a good job of hiding it.

***

I feel slightly bloated after all that bread as I push Ellen further along the High Street towards the solicitors. This time it's Ellen who is in charge, as she is obviously well known by some of the staff there. We're shown into a small side room and I assume it's either Mr Pearce, Legg or Wayburn who follows us in and closes the door behind us.

"Ellen. How lovely to see you again."

The man has slicked back hair, is unctuous, and is a proper dick to boot. Straight away I don't like him, but Ellen obviously does and so I have to go along with it.

"Hello Richard, it's been too long. Tom, this is Richard Wayburn. Richard, this is my husband-to-be, Tom Hopkins."

"Congratulations." Richard Wayburn's arm suddenly extends towards me. "This is a total surprise. When is the happy day?"

"It's a nice surprise to me too." I shake the clammy hand. "We're keeping the date secret."

I hope Ellen picks up on my last remark. She and Wayburn start to talk about the long dead Ken, and I switch off for a moment and look around the room. It's just a functional space, with a table and chairs in the middle where we can sit. There's a painting on one wall showing a rather elderly gentleman in a black suit who wears a cravat over a white shirt with a winged collar. Dick breaks off the conversation and follows my gaze.

"That's James Pearce, our founder. No longer with us unfortunately, but we decided to keep the name. Now Ellen, what can I do for you?"

"I want to make a will before we go on a cruise for our honeymoon. I want to leave everything to Tom, and that's about it. If I outlive Tom, then everything is to go to Cancer Research."

"Well, you're very direct."

"That's me."

"And er… anything to Robert?"

"No, just Tom."

Dick's obviously sized me up as the greatest gold-digger this planet has ever produced. There's definitely something unpleasant about him that I can't put my finger on. I decide to put the record straight.

"This is all Ellen's idea by the way … just so you know."

"I'm sure you'll both be very happy together. I'll take your details, Tom. Ellen and I will draw up the will together, and then I'll bring a couple of staff members in to act as witnesses when we're done. I'll give Ellen a rough copy, and I'll then send the finished will by recorded mail when you're both home from the cruise.

By the time Ellen has finished listing the contents of her safe deposit boxes, the addresses of her properties currently being rented out, her goods, chattels, antique furniture, and a sizeable amount of money in the bank, I realise why Bastard Bob doesn't want his mother to marry a comparatively impecunious ex-roofer on a modest pension. I realise with a jolt that in a few days' time I'll be heir to Ellen's fortune and will be well on my way to becoming a millionaire twice over. I can't get my head around it.

When we exit the solicitors I'm still waiting for that Candid Camera bloke to jump out at us. Ellen announces she needs to put her copy of the will in her bank's safe deposit box, and after we do that there's still time to visit a travel agent to book a world cruise. People go about their normal business along the High Street, while I, Tom Hopkins, pushing ninety, ex-Navvy and ex-roofer, am on my way to book a 2-month honeymoon in the sun while everyone else on the Island freezes their arses off in what will doubtless be yet another winter of discontent.

"Tom, you'll have to make a will too, you know. If you outlive me…"

"I'll do it when we get back from the cruise. "I push Ellen carefully across the road. "I need to have a little think about it first."

***

Twenty four stops around the world for £14,000 per person, but with a supplement for single occupancy in 2 adjoining cabins. Ellen pays in full as though £30,000 is just pocket money. I don't know what to say, but all I *do* know is that we've got 3 weeks to lie low during November, and then it's a Red Funnel ferry to Southampton to board a Pensioners & Obese cruise ship (my name for it anyway) at the beginning of December. When we get back in the taxi bound for Bembridge and my little sheltered housing flat I'm still worried about Bob, and take a moment to wonder if I'm actually doing the right thing. As though she knows exactly what I'm thinking, Ellen squeezes my hand and takes away any doubt. Time to give the eye clinic, the Bingo, the line dancing and the lonely life I've been living a miss, and get used to the 'new normal'.

In my mind's eye I can see my dad standing before me complaining about his lot and how come my bread always lands jam side up. I'm sure if he'd lived he'd now shake his head and call me *Mister Golden Balls*.

CHAPTER SIXTEEN

Two witnesses passing by are only too pleased to be dragged in to St. Catherine's Ceremony Room off a rainy Newport street to officiate at our humble wedding. Frank and Lewis Marchant had been out to find a new carpet, but we were surprised to discover they had themselves been married in the same venue only six months before. To me they are still in that starry eyed phase as they shake my hand, give Ellen a kiss, and follow us into the building. Two men getting married does not faze me anymore, although it might have done back in the day before I learned to live and let live.

A young couple with their whole life before them exit the marriage room complete with a glut of relatives who hold up mobile phones. Another couple, the girl obviously pregnant, wait nearby for their turn after ours. All I can picture in my mind is a supermarket conveyor belt.

The registrar is seriousness personified, and takes no time at all to pronounce us husband and wife. Frank and Lewis are virtually jumping up and down with excitement, but my mind keeps wandering back to my first wedding and the sight of Jean in all her finery. Ellen wears a cream-coloured woollen suit to protect her from the early November chill, a far cry from Jean's white chiffon and lace creation that her mother had made for our July marriage with around sixty guests, now all dead of course. Remember the film 'Four Weddings and a Funeral?' Well, the dark blue suit that just came out of mothballs has seen five funerals in the past ten years and only one wedding… my own one today. In fact I feel a bit of a fraud here… what the hell have I done? I'm still thinking of my first wedding whilst getting married to my second wife, and Ellen doesn't deserve that.

The marriage certificate is placed in my hand. Frank and Lewis suggest a drink to celebrate, but all I want to do is get back in the taxi and go home for a cup of tea. Ellen looks tired, and I suspect she is worried about Bob.

We push past the pregnant girl, her young man, and what look to be their parents. None of them appear particularly happy. Jean and I tried for years to be where they are now. We wanted a baby but didn't get one, and the young couple got one just like that but do not look too happy about it. Life doesn't seem fair, does it?

"Thanks, Frank and Lewis. "I take time to shake their hands. "When you get to our age you don't have many relatives left."

"We loved being your witnesses." Lewis gives Ellen a hug. "Now we'd better get on and buy our carpet."

"Here…" Ellen searches in her bag, takes out a bank book, and gives Lewis a blank cheque. "Have one on us."

"No, absolutely not." Frank gives it back to Ellen and shakes his head. "We wouldn't dream of such a thing."

The taxi is still waiting for us. We wave goodbye to our witnesses, and climb into the taxi.

"Back to Steyne Road, Bembridge please, near the Co-op."

I still do not want to give out my address, just in case Bob is on the prowl. I look across at Ellen.

"Well, Mrs Hopkins… what have you got to say?"

"I say thank you, Tom. You've made me a very happy lady."

I hold on to Ellen's hand, just as I used to do in the eye clinic. She dozes during the journey home, while I wonder in all reality how many more years the two of us have got left.

***

Warden Penny is in her office and sticks her head out of the door as we make our way along the communal corridor to my flat.

"Does your friend still want the guest suite for a few more days?"

"She's not my *friend*, Ellen is now my wife." I grin at Penny. "We've just got married."

"Well… this calls for a celebration!" Penny looks from me to Ellen. "What do you say?"

"No, we just want to celebrate on our own." Ellen shakes her head. "And I still want the guest suite."

There goes my dream (or is it a nightmare?) of a rocking and rolling wedding night. Still, I'm not sure I'll be 'up to it' at my age anyway. Ellen follows me into the flat just as my landline phone rings.

"Switch the kettle on please, Ellen, and I'll just see who's calling."

Not many people ring me anymore. All I can think of is maybe the eye clinic want me to do some work. I hurry to the living room and pick up the receiver.

"Hello."

"Tom Hopkins?"

"Yes."

"You think you've got away with it, but I have friends in high places."

My blood runs cold. How the hell did Bastard Bob get my number? I swallow my fear and decide to play him at his own game.

"I haven't got away with anything, Bob. You're just pissed off because you're not in the will."

"Enjoy your cruise."

The phone goes dead. My hand shakes as I replace the receiver. There's only one other person who could have known about our forthcoming wedding and cruise so soon…the one I've just given all my contact details to.

***

The kettle comes to the boil as I make my way back into the kitchen. Ellen sits at the table in her wedding suit, and seems as stunned as I feel.

"That was Bob."

"Oh?" Ellen looks up at me. "What did he want? How did he find your number? I have my diary here with me, and I'm sure he hasn't seen it."

"He told me I haven't got away with it, and that he has friends in high places. He then said to enjoy the cruise before slamming the phone down."

"He went to the same school as Richard Wayburn… that's how he knows. They've been friends for years, but I didn't realise *how* friendly." Ellen sighs and appears near to tears. "It makes me glad I didn't give him anything in my will."

"Perhaps we should have gone to a different solicitor."

"I don't know any other. I always trusted Richard, and so did Ken. Something tells me Bob might turn up *here*. I'll have to phone him."

"If I were you, I wouldn't. He's angry right now. I'll go and tell Penny not to let him in. There's always somebody in the office, day or night. She'll know to keep the door locked. Hopefully he won't come here before we go away."

I make us a cup of tea and get out the biscuits for a sugar rush, as my muscles seem to have locked up with tension. As I swallow a custard cream whole I cannot help wondering if I've made the biggest mistake of my life.

***

It's the morning after the night before. Ellen is no doubt still asleep in the guest suite, and I'm lying in bed; not in the arms of my wife, but alone and on edge in case Bob calls again or rings the doorbell. I think it might be time to find a hotel near to the port of Southampton, where we can stay in peace until we're allowed to board our cruise ship at the beginning of December.

My brain is firing on all cylinders, making sleep impossible. I wrench the covers over to one side and climb out of bed. Two cups of coffee only add to the jitters. When I hear a light tap on the door I almost jump out of my seat.

"Coo-ee, it's only me." Ellen's voice floats through the letterbox. "Can I come in?"

I'm naked under my dressing gown. I pull the cord a little tighter around my middle. Will she run screaming from the room at the sight of my hairy, veined legs? Still barefoot, I take a chance and pad towards the front door.

"You're up early." I open the door and decide not to apologise for my lack of suitable attire. "Enter, if you dare."

"I dare… I'm made of strong stuff." Ellen, immaculately dressed as usual, giggles and pushes her walker into the passageway. "I couldn't sleep much. Could you?"

"No, I laid awake thinking we ought to stay a few nights in Southampton."

"That's a good idea." Ellen nods. "I've spoken to the matron in my care home and told her I'm married, but not where I'm staying. Nobody will know *where* we are if we book a hotel in Southampton. We'll need to find a travel agent to help us."

"I should have got my head around mobile phones." I sigh. "You see the young folks doing all sorts of things on them. If I'd taken the time and effort to learn, then who knows, I might have been able to book a hotel without even leaving this flat."

"Don't worry… we can get a taxi to Ryde and find a travel agent there." Ellen waves away my frustration with one hand. "The best thing about being mobile phone free is that nobody, not even Bob, can contact us."

I can only agree. Relieved at finding a solution to the ever-present problem of Bob, I pour a cup of coffee out for Ellen and then head towards the kitchen door.

"Help yourself to some cereal and toast. I'm just going to get washed and dressed."

I hum a tune as I shave. The two of us might be old and not too au fait with today's technology, but maybe the old fashioned ways are still the best.

***

It's a blustery morning as the taxi pulls away and I push Ellen in the wheelchair a little way up the long hill of Union Street until thankfully I see a travel agency without having to go all the way to the top. I'm desperate for a coffee, so I leave Ellen to book us a hotel while I slip next door to Costa. The girl behind the counter asks if I 'have the app'. I have no idea what she means, and it's on the tip of my tongue to reply that I always walk that way. Somehow I think my humour will be lost on her.

CHAPTER SEVENTEEN

Ellen of course has booked the best two rooms in the hotel, both of which have stunning views of Southampton's Calshot Beach and the Solent. Unfortunately, it's far too cold to hire deckchairs and feel the sand under our toes. Also, due to the time of year the hotel seems half empty, which actually suits both of us.

On that first day we sit safe behind large patio doors in my overly-warm room and gaze out to sea. I take hold of Ellen's hand.

"You and me against the world, eh?"

"Or just against Bob." Ellen chuckles.

"Didn't the two of you ever get on?"

"Tom, you don't know the whole story. Ever since I've been a widow he's been sickly sweet, but at the same time he goes on and on at me to make a will. He's even said several times that he's going to drive me to see Richard Wayburn. I'm not stupid and I've known for years what he's after. However, I'm a stubborn old woman, and he's not getting a penny. It's not that we were ever close… he used to give me hell as a teenager and it got to the point where I hated the sight of him."

"I'm so sorry to hear this." I squeeze Ellen's fingers. "A mother and her son should have a special relationship. I loved my old mum, bless her. Wasn't so keen on Dad though."

"In theory, yes it should be special, but in reality when you have kids of your own it can be somewhat different."

There it is again… the little dig I often come across from people who say I don't know what I'm talking about because I've never been a parent, and now Ellen's doing it. It's supposed to be our honeymoon, and so I choose to ignore her remark and decide instead to change the subject.

"Just think… if I hadn't decided to do some voluntary work at the eye clinic, we would never have met."

"I used to sit in the waiting area and listen to the old ladies talking about someone in the clinic who holds their hands. You were the man for me, because you took my fingers in a gentle kind of grasp and put me at ease straight away."

"Now I've got the same problem as you, but not as bad." I chuckle. "Who holds the hand of the hand-holder when it comes to *my* turn?"

"*Me* of course, silly." Ellen looks at me with some incredulity. "Your wife. Who else?"

"How did you know I was *available*, so to speak?"

"My dear Tom, if you'd still been married to Jean you'd have had no need to hold other ladies' hands."

She is right of course. A smattering of sleet hits the window pane in front of me while I cogitate on how Jean and I would have spent our twilight years enjoying each other's company as we schlepped around garden centres and DIY stores. I still find it difficult to believe that Jean is gone and I am now married to Ellen. It all seems to have happened so fast.

"Perhaps men don't fare as well as women when they're left on their own."

A red funnelled ferry sails across the Solent bound for East Cowes, while Madeira awaits Ellen and me in just a few days' time. I have to start living in the present and stop thinking about the past. Time to enjoy what little time I have left upon this earth.

***

I climb out of the taxi and strain my neck upwards. I have never in my life seen such a huge and majestic-looking ship. At least 14 decks stretch upwards towards the sky. I then turn from left to right and take in the colossal length of it. This is a bit of an upgrade from the Isle of Wight ferry.

"Wow!"

I'm stumped for any more words. I even forget to pay the taxi driver, and so Ellen does it.

"Come on, Tom. Time to broaden your horizons a bit."

There's a Salvation Army band playing Christmas carols on the dock. They must be freezing their nuts off... the women as well. Efficient as usual, Ellen has already arranged for a porter to help us, who makes his way over to the taxi.

"Mr and Mrs Hopkins?"

"That's us." I decide we must stick out a mile, as no other passengers except we two could look so old. "I can push my wife in the wheelchair, if you would kindly take our luggage and my wife's walker."

"Of course. If you make your way towards the marquee near the band and join the *Access* queue, then you'll be signed in and given your boarding pass in no time at all. Your luggage and walker will be delivered to your cabin."

I want to take a moment to remind the porter that we have two adjoining cabins, but he's already gone on young legs as long as drainpipes. All around us there's a bustle of people hurrying this way and that, while the band plays Good King Wenceslas as loud as they can over people's voices and the sound of lorries backing up after delivering pallets of tinned and fresh foodstuffs to the waiting ship's crew. I can't help but feel a twinge of excitement. Mother would have said that people like me don't usually get to travel on cruise ships, and people like me have to be satisfied with a deckchair on Ryde beach. I can't take in what's happened in such a short space of time.

"Haven't you ever been on a cruise, Tom?" Jean looks up at me from over her right shoulder. "You look all at sea, so to speak, and we haven't even got on the ship yet."

"Never." I push the wheelchair towards the marquee. "I'm afraid I'm not very well travelled."

"There'll always be something to do or somewhere to visit. Anyway, it'll take you a month to find your way around the ship in the first place."

***

A very nice chap will look after us and clean our cabins. Ravi is from Goa, and already he's falling over himself to serve us. He even helps Ellen to unpack. We settle in and then it's a bit of a trek up to the buffet restaurant on Deck 13, but I manage to find the lift and push Ellen there in her wheelchair. Firstly we're confronted with a member of the crew spraying everyone's hands with sanitiser, and then we're shown a confusing amount of hot and cold food, all set out on different counters.

"Tom, this place is filling up with people. I'll bag a table if you can bring me some soup and a sandwich."

I'm not sure where the sandwiches might be, or even if I'll find Ellen again once I've done the rounds. I don't recognise half of the stuff on offer, and all I want is beans on toast. I realise the ship is moving while crowds gather around each counter, and I end up with green- coloured wraps with a kind of ham and rice filling… at least that's what I *think* it is. I also grab 2 slices of lemon cake nearby. I cannot carry drinks as well, and so I look around for Ellen.

"Can I help you, Sir?"

I must look bloody demented to the crew member, who stands there and smiles at me. There are tables all around the restaurant, and everywhere people walk in front, to the side, and behind me carrying trays of food.

"Just getting my bearings. I'll be all right in a minute."

I'm too embarrassed to say that I'm lost. I turn this way and that. To my relief I see Ellen, who stands up and waves.

"You've been ages." Ellen gives the evil eye to a plateful of green wraps. "What are they?"

"I don't know. Just try them. I couldn't find any sandwiches. I'll go and find some drinks and then come back."

"When I return carrying 2 mugs of coffee, Ellen has eaten all the wraps."

"They were okay, whatever they were."

"But some were for me! Now I've got to go and get more."

"Sorry. You didn't say."

Maybe with enough trips to the buffet tables I might be able to find my way back to my seat before it's time to disembark. It's all very confusing. The ship is so big that it's going to take me the rest of my time here to learn where everything is. When I get out of the dining area I've got to try and remember where our cabins are.

"Ellen, do you know how to get back again?"

"Normally you follow the right coloured carpet. Our corridor on Deck Eight has a blue one because it's in the middle of the ship. That's what I remember from previous holidays."

"That's a start, anyway."

I haven't even noticed the carpets, let alone what colour they are. I've got a lot to learn about cruise ships.

CHAPTER EIGHTEEN

I sit in Funchal's Botanical Gardens, Madeira. It's the first excursion on the itinerary, and the weather is fortunately quite mild at 20 degrees. Ellen has stayed in a tea room below, as it's a steep climb uphill and I don't think I could have managed to push the wheelchair. This hill is worse than Union Street. There are a few other passengers that have also chickened out for her to talk to there, and so I'm not worried.

I'm a bit winded, but I enjoyed the cable car ride over the ravine, and I'm glad I made it to the gardens to enjoy the native flora and fauna laid out there and of course a spectacular view over the Atlantic Ocean in the background. It's all a bit different from the Isle of Wight, although it seems there are just as many hills. The sun is warm on my face, and I relax a bit.

I wake up with a jolt and finish my bottle of water. I must have dozed off for a moment. Ellen will be wondering where I am.

I can see others from our group as they make their way down to where the coach waits. I know they're from our excursion, as we all wear the same red stickers on our tops that make us stand out like sore thumbs. To me these stickers scream 'Mug Me!', but the guide seems to want us to wear them.

I stand up and shake out my stiff legs. You'd have thought I'd be used to hills, but these ones are of the industrial kind. Another old boy with a red sticker falls in beside me and we make idle chat as we walk slowly downwards while holding onto the railings provided for dear life.

Ellen has already been helped onto the coach, and she waves to me from her window seat. I haul myself up the first step, and give a sigh of relief as I sit beside her.

"What was it like?"

"Lovely gardens and views, but very steep hills."

"Perhaps it's better I didn't go then."

She lets me sleep a bit on the way back. That trek took more out of me than I care to admit. Next time I'm going to check the terrain before I make another venture off the ship.

***

The end of another day in paradise. We docked this morning at Las Palmas, but some way out because there's too many cruise ships in the port. We have to wait until tomorrow to dock properly. Passengers can still visit places, and little orange tenders go back and forth to shore all the time. However, we've both been happy to remain on board and sit on the deck. Ellen's been reading a lot today, but now she's decided to go into her cabin for a doze before dinner. I'm quite wide awake after hours of not doing much. I turn on the TV just as I hear a knock on my cabin door. I whistle and peep through the security spyhole, but stop short at the face framed in the glass. I assume I've made a mistake and open the door for confirmation. However, no mistake has been made. Bob stands before me, his features contorted into a rather angry kind of grimace.

"Bob? What the hell are *you* doing here?"

I blink in confusion as Bob barges in and then shuts the door with his foot.

"Let's say I want to set all the records straight."

"But... how did you get here? How did you know we were on board? We didn't see you at Southampton."

Something's not right, and hackles have already gone up on the back of my neck. A shiver of fear runs through me which I try to control. I want to get out into the corridor, but Bob blocks my exit. I start to sidle over to the inter-connecting door.

"I joined the ship when it reached Madeira. It's always good to know the right kind of people that can help me keep tags on the pair of you."

Richard Wayburn springs to mind straight away, with his unctuous charm. I move a bit faster, but now Bob already stands between myself and the relative safety of Ellen's cabin.

"There's no way you're going to inherit my mother's money. You know that, don't you?"

"Tough titty. I've *already* inherited it."

For a split second I enjoy winding him up, but now up close and personal I can see his eyes are bulging with hatred. I've had a good life, but now I think it's over; just like *that* it's come to an end. I shout out Ellen's name to no avail just as Bob's fat fist makes painful contact with my right eye, sending me hurtling backwards.

CHAPTER NINETEEN

ELLEN

I wake up with a start, confused. Outside is pitch dark, and the ship's engines are silent. We must still be moored at Las Palmas. Next stop Cape Verde in 2 days' time. Feeling somewhat hungry, I reach over and turn on the bedside light. It's eight o'clock in the evening and it appears I've slept for four hours. I'm angry that Tom hasn't woken me up for dinner.

With some difficulty I sit up and take a deep breath.

"Tom!"

I call his name twice more, but the door between our cabins remains firmly closed. I grab my walker and with my usual sloth-like pace go towards the door, which isn't locked. I slide it back. The TV and spotlights are on, the curtains are drawn, but there's no sign of Tom. I just *know* he would not have gone to dinner without me. All I can assume is that he has toddled off for a walk whilst waiting for me to wake up.

I decide to have a wash and a change of clothes in the meantime. However, when I exit the bathroom half an hour later and take a peep into his cabin, there's still no sign of him.

I'm slightly worried now.

I dial the number given on the internal phone to summon a member of staff, and then open the main door and look out into the corridor. Within a few minutes the lovely Ravi arrives.

"Can I help you, Mrs Ellen?"

"Ravi, I don't know where my husband is." My legs feel like jelly and I hurry as fast as I can back into the cabin and flop down on a nearby chair. "He's disappeared. I don't know if he's gone up to the restaurant. I haven't had any dinner and I can't get up to the buffet on my own. He usually pushes me in the wheelchair."

"I'm sure that's where he'll be." Ravi is all smiles. "Would you like me to bring you something to eat?"

"Yes that would be nice. Something like fish and chips please. Could you look out for him? Do you know Mister Tom? Do you clean *his* cabin?"

"Yes, I clean all the cabins along this corridor. I will bring dinner to you and will have a look for Mister Tom in the restaurant. I would not be allowed to push you in a wheelchair."

Perhaps I'm just an old lady panicking over nothing, but I have a sense of unease that will not go away. Tom is behaving rather strangely, and I know he would never usually leave me to sit in the cabin all evening on my own. Something is wrong, I know it.

Ravi returns with a meal on a tray. I sit at my dressing table and lift the lid on exquisitely presented cod, chips and peas, with apple pie and custard for pudding.

"Thank you so much. Did you find Mister Tom?"

"Sorry, but I did not. I'm sure he will be back soon."

Ravi disappears to carry out his evening duties. My appetite slowly fades, but I push the food down my throat anyway. I make a decision that if Tom has not returned in the next 60 minutes then I will make another phone call, but this time to the people on Reception duty to see what advice they can give me. The hot chips have a calming effect, but all the while I'm eating I cannot help but wonder where the hell my husband might be.

***

Exactly one hour later the chips have settled like concrete in my stomach, and my hand shakes as I pick up the phone again. A friendly female voice trills in my ear, and I try not to let my voice falter.

"Hello. This is Caron. How may I help you?"

"Caron, this is Ellen Hopkins from Cabin seventy four. I want to report that my husband, Tom Hopkins, has disappeared. He's been gone for quite a few hours now and I'm very worried. I don't know what to do next."

"Are you sure that he hasn't just gone off for a walk?"

"I'm certain. I'm quite elderly and disabled, and he wouldn't have left me alone for such a long time."

"Did you say your husband's name is Tom Hopkins?"

"Yes."

"Hold on a moment… a bell is ringing in my head. I just need to have a chat with one of my colleagues."

Maddening musak assaults my ears, the kind you hear in supermarkets. All I want to know is where Tom is. It's an age before the receptionist comes back to me.

"Sorry to have been gone so long, Mrs Hopkins. I needed to check with the member of staff who worked the previous shift. She remembers that your son boarded the ship at Madeira and then arrived at the reception desk. He didn't know your cabin number and wanted to surprise you for your wedding anniversary. The member of staff told him the numbers of yours and your husband's cabins. Happy anniversary by the way. Your son gave all the right answers to questions I asked him regarding your name, address, and date of birth. He even had a photo in his wallet of you sitting next to him, which matched the features we have of you from the photo we took when you embarked.

Deep in my chest I can feel my heartbeat pick up speed.

"It can't be my son. He hasn't been in to see me. He hasn't phoned my cabin."

There's one of those heavy pregnant pauses on the other end, while my heart runs the equivalent of the London Marathon.

"I'll send somebody from Security along to your cabin, Mrs Hopkins. Don't worry. We'll find your husband."

I replace the receiver and sit in a kind of stupefied silence until I hear a light tap on the door. I stand up on legs that feel as though they don't belong to me, grab my frame, and make sure to look through the spyhole first. A man in uniform stands on the other side. It's not Bob. I turn the handle and come face to face with a giant about six feet six in height.

"Mrs Hopkins. I'm Raymond Weldon, Head of Security. Call me *Ray*. You have reported that your husband is missing?"

"Yes. Please come in. I've a bad feeling about all of this."

I turn around to go back to my seat. Ray closes the door and manoeuvres the only other chair available so he can sit facing me.

"First of all I'll show you the photo of the man who claims he is your son. Security took this photo when he boarded at Madeira."

Ray taps something on his mobile phone and then holds the screen nearer to me. I gasp to see Bob smiling back as though he hasn't got a care in the world.

"Yes, that's Bob, but I'm not sure how he knew we were here. I made a point of not telling him where we were going."

"Has he contacted you on board?"

"No, not at all. I don't want to see him either. If you ask me, Bob's got something to do with Tom going missing. You see, we've only just got married. Bob tried to keep us apart because he wants to inherit my estate, but I made a will before we went away leaving everything to Tom."

This man is big and broad enough to take my worries upon his shoulders and search the ship from top to bottom. I really don't want to think about what Bob might have done.

"You won't see your son on board, Mrs Hopkins. He disembarked earlier this evening. We took back his boarding pass as he went through security. Something about a family crisis, an emergency, and that he was wanted at home."

"Was his wife with him?"

"No, he was on his own."

At least I am safe for the moment. Thinking about it, Bob would not have thrown me overboard as he would not have wanted to wait the regulation seven years for me to be declared dead if I hadn't washed up on any foreign shore. Taking into consideration the state of me, I've probably got less than seven years left to live anyway. With a jolt of surprise I remember that if Tom is dead then Cancer Research is now my main beneficiary, and I have the rough draft of my will locked in a special bank deposit box to prove it.

"Ray, we need to get the police involved. I think he might have murdered my husband."

"Let's not jump to conclusions." Ray stands up and pockets his phone. "I'll search your son's and your husband's cabins right now to start with and take it from there."

Deep down in my soul I know I'll never see Tom again, and this cruise has lost its allure without him. We didn't know each other for very long, but he was a kind man and we had so many plans for our future together. I want to cry a river, but right now that will not help. Bob needs to be arrested for what he has undoubtedly done.

The cabin seems very empty once Ray leaves, and my mind goes into overdrive. Tom is gone; I'm suddenly overwhelmed, and have no idea how I'm going to get home all by myself. However, I must stay strong and keep going for Tom's sake. I mustn't collapse like some Victorian maiden whose corsets are too tight.

CHAPTER TWENTY

No sign of Tom has been found, of course. Ray and his team discovered evidence of what might have been blood stains in Tom's cabin, but the carpet had been cleaned and indeed was still wet. In my heart of hearts I know any further searching would be fruitless because my lovely husband now lies at the bottom of the Atlantic. My hope is that his body might wash ashore somewhere, but I expect Bob is astute enough to have made sure, under the cover of darkness, that this would never happen.

Ray gets the local coastguard involved early next morning, and a search helicopter flies overhead as the ship moves further in towards the port now that a space has become available.

I don't know what to do next. I'm like two of those three monkeys… I've seen and heard nothing. Ravi brings me some breakfast, and almost as soon as I've had a wash there's a knock on my cabin door. Ray stands there accompanied by a middle-aged man wearing some kind of uniform.

"Mrs Hopkins, I have Agente Martin Lopez with me, an officer in the local police force. He's here to ask you some questions about your son."

I have been expecting this. With so much grief and anger churning around in my body I didn't sleep much at all last night. I am eager to answer his questions.

"Come in, please."

There are only two chairs. I sink into the most comfortable one, Agente Lopez takes the other one, and Ray sits on the bed.

"Mrs Hopkins, please call me *Martin.* First of all I am so sorry that your husband has disappeared."

Martin's accent is easy to understand, and he sounds genuinely sympathetic. I like him straight away.

"I feel very strongly that he's disappeared because I'm sure my son Bob has murdered him and then obviously chucked his body overboard. According to the security computers, is my husband still on board?"

"Yes. He has not disembarked."

Tears sting the back of my eyes as I think of Tom. I blink them away and focus on the job in hand.

"Why do you think your husband has been murdered?"

"Ray tells me that Bob boarded the ship when we docked in Madeira, and then he disembarked yesterday evening. Security cameras and his boarding pass card must have verified this. Yesterday evening is when Tom went missing. Bob never got in touch with me while he was here, and then he was gone on some jumped up excuse of an emergency at home. Someone on Reception gave him Tom's cabin number. Bob is very angry that Tom and I got married, and he tried to stop us as he wants to be the main beneficiary of my will."

"And he's not?"

"No. It'll all go to Cancer Research now unless Tom is found, but it's in Bob's nature to contest the will, and I'm sure he'll do so. He's got friends in the legal world who will help him to get what he wants, I'm sure."

Martin makes some notes on his phone, and then turns to Ray. This makes me wonder whether anybody uses a pen and paper at all these days.

"Mister Weldon, you've done a thorough search of the adjoining cabin and of the ship?"

"Of course." Ray nods. "I had my team searching long into the night."

"We've put Gran Canaria Airport on red alert in case he tries to fly out, and have also alerted the ferry companies. The security photo we took of him has been circulated far and wide." Martin leans forward in my direction. "We will find him and question him. We've also alerted the UK airports."

"Knowing Bob, he would have probably chartered a boat. He's very resourceful. He had a bit of time to get away, and he's not stupid. I was asleep and didn't realise Tom was missing for four hours. Bob could be anywhere by now."

"So you've never had an ideal relationship with your son?" Ray shifts about on the bed to sit more upright. "You've never been close?"

"Not really." I shake my head. "His father spoilt him when he was a child, and it was always *me* who had to come down harder on him. I ended up rather disliking him actually, especially when he'd try and suck up to me to get what he wanted. He still does it as an adult, but I can always see through *that*. Let's just say we're not bosom buddies."

"Thank you for the information." Martin stands up. "We'll keep you informed. We'll also get Forensics in to check the carpet stains next door."

"I – I don't want to stay on the ship." I heave a sigh with shaky breath. "Tom's not coming back and I want to go home. I have the wherewithal to pay for somebody to assist me back to the UK. Is that possible?"

"Yes, we can do that for you, but just stay a while longer while we carry out our investigations. In the meantime we can organise your disembarkation and a flight home from Cape Verde in say, a week's time." Ray gets to his feet and stands next to Martin. "How does that grab you?"

"You're very kind." I nod. "Thank you."

I'm left with a hollow feeling inside as the two men leave. I don't want to go out of the cabin for the rest of the week and see all the loved-up couples strolling arm-in-arm around the promenade deck or having cosy chats in the lounges. In the privacy of my cabin I look down at my shiny new wedding ring and let the river of tears fall which I have so far managed to keep at bay. As I suspected, I feel no better for it.

CHAPTER TWENTY ONE

The search for Tom was called off after seven days and he is missing presumed dead, although nobody wants to say the latter conclusion to my face. Spatterings of his blood was found by Forensics. I haven't been out of my cabin for a whole week. Ravi is kindness personified and has brought me any meals I wanted. Bob has not been sighted anywhere.

With Ray's help I manage to phone Trish, and all she can tell me is that Bob is on the mainland on business. I have a feeling that's all she knows. I tell her how he'd turned up on the ship and how the police are now looking for him on account of Tom's disappearance. She sounds quite shocked on hearing this. The shock seems genuine.

Ray's wife Shirley works in the ship's hairdressing salon and has volunteered for the onerous task of getting me back to the Isle of Wight. I give my bank card to Shirley and she books our direct flights to Heathrow and then another flight for her back to Grantley Adams' airport, Barbados, which will give her time to get to the next port of call after Cape Verde. She also books the Wightlink ferry for us as foot passengers. I didn't know there was another way of doing all this apart from going into a travel agency. Shirley says that hopefully I might be able to claim some money back on the holiday when I get home.

It's with a heavy heart that I say goodbye to Ravi and Ray and let Shirley wheel me down the gangplank at Porto Grande, Mindelo, in order to take a taxi to Cesaria Evora airport and start our trek back to the UK, where I've discovered the temperature there is 2 degrees Centigrade. Here it's 25 degrees, and Tom and I should be having a wonderful time in the sun. I'm so angry at what's happened that I have nothing left but loathing for Bob. The UK police are searching for him, but as of now I have no husband and no son anymore. I am alone in the world apart from my friends at the care home. I will need to sort out Tom's affairs when I get back, but at the moment I have a long journey ahead of me and I can't think too much about that. Ray has kindly organised for Tom's luggage to be packed up and sent back to his address in Bembridge, as it would be too much for Shirley to deal with as well as mine. I will need to think about what I'm going to do with his effects.

Shirley is kind, upbeat and garrulous, but her constant talking grates on my nerves. I know she's trying to distract me from my grief, and so I make a point of trying to be interested in what she has to say. It's so tiring to listen to somebody who has a chronic case of verbal diarrhoea. I wish I could do all this travelling by myself, but I'm too old and infirm now.

I feign sleep on the plane for at least half of the six hour flight, and Shirley shuts up. It's still dark when we arrive at Heathrow, and I've lost track of what day or time it is. All I know is that thankfully I've missed Christmas and that it's nearly January. Shirley collects the luggage and then wheels me to a taxi rank outside, where another cheerful person is only too happy to drive us to Gunwharf Quay at Portsmouth. There's a high wind and the ferry crossing is rather rough. Shirley disappears to the toilet, but I stay sitting in my wheelchair at a middle table. I don't care about the rolling ferry. I've got nothing to live for now, and so if the boat sinks then so be it.

It's only polite to offer Shirley the guest suite to stay in overnight. However, she seems anxious to get away, and to be honest, I just want to be left alone to remember Tom and the brief time we had together. Matron knocks and helps me to unpack, and I tell her what I know so far. She says she will no longer follow any of Bob's instructions and will re-install my landline phone, but still I'm rather pleased when she goes away.

I pick up a souvenir menu that Shirley had put in my case, and the straight edges seem bent. The words are not easy to read. On top of everything that's happened it looks as though I might need another course of Lucentis injections as well. What's the point of crying about it? No point at all in fact. Nobody's here to comfort me… and so I might as well just get on with it.

***

The next day I pluck up courage to phone Trish again. She still has not heard from Bob, and her anger at him is apparent by the tone of her voice. She has already investigated Bob's whereabouts on the mainland where he was supposed to be, and has discovered he has not been seen or heard of. I feel a small tingle of triumph run up my spine as I now know she believes every word I've been saying. Due to his lies and now lack of trust she thinks he must have another woman somewhere who is hiding him, and it sounds as though Bob and Trish's marriage might be floundering on the rocks. To my surprise Trish asks whether she can come for a visit.

***

It's a bit awkward at first. Trish plonks herself down on the chair that Tom once sat upon, and neither of us know what to say as we've never been that friendly. However, my daughter-in-law soon finds her voice.

"I never knew that Bob had boarded the ship. Hope you believe me."

"I do." I nod. "He's deceived both of us."

"The police have visited me."

"Yes, I expect they would have. I told them I think Bob murdered Tom and threw his body overboard. He still won't get my money though, as I've left it to Cancer Research."

"Good for you." Trish smiles at me. "You've had the last laugh."

"I'm not laughing much though."

"I'm sorry for what he's done to you, Ellen." Trish gets to her feet, walks towards me, then perches on the arm of my chair and puts one arm around my shoulders. "You don't deserve this."

Human contact; the warmth of Trish's arm and her unexpected comforting touch threaten another storm of tears, but that's the last thing she would want. I lean in and enjoy the closeness of what may now be the only relative I have left that might want to pay another visit.

"When you last saw Bob, did he tell you when he was coming home?"

"That date has come and gone. We hadn't been getting on that well to tell you the truth. As I told you on the phone, I've suspected for a long time that he has another woman on the go."

"I'm not sure what else we can do, Trish. We have to leave things to the police now. It's embarrassing to see my son's face on the TV news bulletins. I'm sure all the grandchildren are appalled too."

"I don't think the news has reached Stuart in Sydney yet, but I'm sure the girls will tell him soon enough. Funny, but I can't bring myself to let him know. It'll kill the image he has of his father."

"Bob's let us all down big time." I reach up and take hold of Trish's fingers. "I didn't get on with him much, but I never thought he'd do something like this."

"It just goes to show what people will do for money."

We sit in a kind of companionable silence for a while, each with our own thoughts. Presently Trish stands up.

"I'll put the kettle on. Isn't tea supposed to be the universal panacea?"

"Huh. I've always preferred coffee."

I wait for Trish to return. At the same time I watch out for Bob to burst in and demand that Trish leaves straight away, like he did with Tom and anyone else brave enough to stay for tea. As I chat to Trish I realise I actually like my daughter-in-law, who seems quite a different person now that she is free from Bob.

I wonder what on earth I did wrong as a mother.

CHAPTER TWENTY TWO

THREE MONTHS' LATER

An appointment for the eye clinic drops onto my mat together with the final printed will. I carefully check that Richard Wayburn has not altered any wording, and make a mental note to ask Trish for a lift into Newport the next time she goes there so that I can place it into my safe deposit box. I'm thinking of making her the executor, even though she isn't a beneficiary. That's not to say I might make changes in time and bequeath her some jewellery as well. She's been good to me since I lost Tom. We've both suffered a loss of a loved one in one way or another, and it's brought us closer together.

Trish was correct in that Bob had found somebody else; this time a seasoned sailor and free spirit called Susan Jenkins, based in the Las Palmas area and living most of the time on her own boat. He had visited a nightclub on that fateful evening, drunk a lot, met Susan, and she had taken him on board. Bob's charm soon won Susan over. However, she had decided to do the right thing and inform the police when she saw Bob's picture in one of the English newspapers when going ashore to pick up supplies. She had wondered why Bob had always been unwilling to go ashore and had more often than not stayed below deck. By then there was a reward of £50,000, put up by myself, for anybody with any genuine information about the case. Susan claimed it. I hope it does her some good.

As for Bob, he was extradited back to the UK and arrested and charged as soon as his plane reached Heathrow. He denies everything of course, but after trolling through hours of security CCTV on the ship, one camera at the end of the corridor captured him standing outside Tom's cabin on the night he disappeared and then going inside. I suspect a jury won't take long to make up their minds.

***

And now another appointment for the eye clinic has come around. It was a shock to see my old surname on the letter, and realise with everything that's happened that I've forgotten to inform the hospital of the change. Matron has been kind enough to order a taxi and to send Lesley, one of the care assistants with me for support. I don't fancy going back there if truth be told, because memories of Tom are still too fresh, but of course needs must.

We have time for a trip to the café first, and I make sure I sit in the same chair that Tom did on that last occasion we were there together. I'd like to think some of his DNA might have been left in some hard-to-find recess somewhere. However, Lesley's inane chatter cuts off most of my thoughts, and there's just time to slosh down a cup of coffee and eat a sticky bun.

I give my new surname to the girl on the clinic reception desk. I still haven't got used to it myself, but it will be a lasting reminder of Tom. I'm not too keen on injections from Mister Joe, and would have preferred the lady doctor. Lesley says she will stay in the waiting room until I come out, and when the nurse calls my name I make my way slowly into the consulting room. There's no chair by the treatment table anymore where Tom used to sit, and it's just Mister Joe, myself, and one nurse in the room.

I've had lots of these injections before and I know the drill. I lie down on the treatment table, put my hands by my side, and suffer the numbing local anaesthetic. However, the clinic must have a new hand-holder because all of a sudden somebody's warm fingers encircle my left hand and give it a squeeze. The nurse is over to my right sorting out the injection. I wasn't aware that anybody else had come into the room. Maybe the squeeze was rather forward for a first meeting, but hey ho, perhaps I'm being old-fashioned.

When the injection is over the hand-holder is still grasping my fingers, so I'm interested to see who sits next to me. The table is lowered and I raise myself up. The nurse bustles about and Mister Joe washes his hands. I'm surprised to find there is nobody else in the room.

"Who held my hand just now?" My heart beats a tattoo in my chest. I don't like to declare that whoever it was is still doing so.

"Nobody, Mrs Hopkins." The nurse shakes her head. "We haven't had anyone here for ages. I think you must have been imagining it."

Well, that's where she's wrong. I *know* what I felt, and still feel. Tentatively I give the hand a squeeze, and am rewarded with the same. I climb off the bed, grab my walker, and the disembodied fingers now rest on top of my left hand.

I smile to nobody in particular, because I'm happy that I've found him at long last … I've found my Tom. He's still holding my hand from beyond his watery grave, and there's no other explanation for it. Love never dies. I'll sleep better in my bed tonight knowing that although Tom's body is fodder for the fishes, his spirit will always be here with me.

CHAPTER TWENTY THREE

TOM – ONE YEAR LATER

I like to sit in God's garden. It's out of this world, because I can't put a name to any of the flowers here, which glow with colours I've never seen before. Jean, young and vibrant, sits on one side of me on a wooden bench, and Ellen sits on the other side. I hold both their hands; I've got two wives, but neither wife seems too keen on speaking to the other one. The large dent in my head from hitting the side of a table has gone, and so has the ache in my legs. My brother, aunts and uncles, cousins, even my parents and grandparents, stroll past on a regular basis and say hello as we sit there. They're all young again. Far from being lonely I'm now surrounded with relatives. It's bloody weird, I can tell you.

Yes, we've all crossed the Styx. Ellen passed away in her sleep (I was with her when she crossed) and now Cancer Research had better come up with something marvellous now they've got all the money that Bob and I never had.

Strangest of all is a man who looks a lot like me and calls me 'Dad'. Jean hadn't even known she'd been pregnant. My grandmother brought him up and called him Philip, after the Duke of Edinburgh, whom she'd always fancied. Philip must be at least fifty but he looks years younger, as he tells me that twenty five is the age he wants to remain at. I didn't even know

I *could* be younger than I am, but it seems that anything is possible on the 'other side'. Yes, as far as I'm concerned twenty five is a good age to be, and so I think of how I was then. Ellen, transformed into a slip of a girl, nods with approval and tells me she's never seen me looking so young and muscly. Jean pipes up and replies that of course *she* has, as she was with me for 65 years and not a mere year or so. I stay out of it and shut up.

I don't need to eat, and tiredness is a thing of the past. My days are spent keeping both wives happy, and getting to know Philip. On the odd occasion when I think of Ellen's son I'm taken to a prison cell where Bob hangs from the neck. Thankfully he hasn't joined us here; Ellen tells me he has to remain in limbo until he comes to terms with what he did and then decides to make amends. This suits me, as I don't want to see him.

I also like to daydream. I've only got to think of my childhood home and I'm there with my brother and Mum as she sings that song about Kathleen. The house is solid. I can even sleep in my old bedroom if I want to, even though I don't need to go to bed now.

It's not too bad being dead. Did Bob do me a favour? I'm not sure about that one as it would be nice to have had a small fortune at my disposal, albeit just for a short time. What would I have done with it? Hmm… it would have made my last days more bearable that's for sure. I could have moved to the BUPA care home in Wroxall and be waited on hand and foot. Knowing me though I'd have ended up doing little jobs around the home for all the ladies for something to do.

But yes, I'm happy in the garden of eternal rest. I'm not complaining. You never know, one day Jean and Ellen might even speak to each other. Until then I'll do the job I'm very good at doing… I'll hold both their hands and hope for the best.

THE END

MORE BOOKS BY STEVIE TURNER

A HOUSE WITHOUT WINDOWS
A LONG SLEEP
A RATHER UNUSUAL ROMANCE
ALYS IN HUNGERLAND
BARREN
CRUISING DANGER
EXAMINING KITCHEN CUPBOARDS
FALLING
FAREWELL
FINDING DAVID: A PARANORMAL SHORT STORY
FOR THE SAKE OF A CHILD
HIS LADYSHIP
LEG-LESS AND CHALAZA
LIFE: 18 SHORT STORIES
LILY: A SHORT STORY
MIND GAMES
NO SEX PLEASE, I'M MENOPAUSAL!
PARTNERS IN TIME
REPENT AT LEISURE
REVENGE
SCAM!
THE DAUGHTER-IN-LAW SYNDROME
THE DONOR
THE NOISE EFFECT
THE PILATES CLASS
TRIO: THREE SHORT STORIES

www.ingramcontent.com/pod-product-compliance
Lightning Source LLC
LaVergne TN
LVHW010626100826
845148LV00014B/3124
* 9 7 8 1 7 3 9 4 0 1 0 8 5 *